Walter Dean Myers

⊷⊶The⊷⊶
RIGHTEOUS
REVENGE
of Artemis Bonner

🔖HarperTrophy®
A Division of HarperCollins*Publishers*

OCT 08

The Righteous Revenge of Artemis Bonner
Copyright © 1992 by Walter Dean Myers
For information address HarperCollins Children's Books,
a division of HarperCollins Publishers,
10 East 53rd Street, New York, NY 10022.

Library of Congress Cataloging-in-Publication Data
Myers, Walter Dean, date
    The righteous revenge of Artemis Bonner / Walter Dean Myers.
        p.   cm.
    Summary: Fifteen-year-old Artemis journeys from New York City
to Tombstone, Arizona, in 1882, to avenge the murder of his uncle.
    ISBN 0-06-020844-9. — ISBN 0-06-020846-5 (lib. bdg.)
    ISBN 0-06-440462-5 (pbk.)
    [1. Revenge—Fiction.   2. Buried treasure—Fiction.   3. West
(U.S.)—Fiction.   4. Afro-Americans—Fiction.]   I. Title.
PZ7.M992Ri   1992   91-42401
[Fic]—dc20   CIP
                                                          AC

First Harper Trophy edition, 1994.
Visit us on the World Wide Web!
http://www.harperchildrens.com

ONE

I, ARTEMIS BONNER, IN ORDER TO get my side of the story on record, and to explain why I am going to kill a low-lifed and sniveling scoundrel called by the name of Catfish Grimes, am writing down my side of the story so the real truth is known. I do not want anyone to think, when the time comes, that Catfish died by accident or by the hand of a stranger. It was me, Artemis Bonner, who has done the deed. By the time this is read, I do believe that the wretched soul of Catfish Grimes will be roasting in Eternal Hell. So be it, and here is the whole story, and the truth as well.

It all started a little over two years ago in the month of May. I was doing what the dear ladies of the Salvation Army call poorly, as I was without regular work in my chosen profession, that of sign painter. At the time I was living in the city of New York, in the state of New York, and had been living there for some fifteen years, or since the day of my birth. I lived with my mother, a beautiful woman as only mothers can be, at number 125 West Fortieth Street.

Father had died two years before and had left but eighteen dollars and forty-two cents behind. Life had not been easy for Mother and me, although I had done well enough in the sign-painting business, being of sure hand and a good speller.

On the day it all started, my mother received a letter from my aunt Mary in Tombstone, Arizona. Most of the letter passed the time of day in polite fashion, as is the custom, inquiring as to our health and well-being and wishing us God's Holy Grace in all our endeavors. But the next part declared the most awful news that I had heard in a long time. Mother called me into the kitchen and sat me down at the table.

"Oh, Son, I have just received the worst news that I can imagine," she said.

I saw the letter in her lap and could not help but notice that her lower lip trembled as she spoke.

I put my hand on the small brown hand of the one person I loved more than any other in the world, and patted it gently.

"Your father's brother, Ugly Ned, has been shot down in the streets of Tombstone," Mother said.

"Has he given up the ghost?" I asked.

"I am afraid so," Mother said, her voice floating into the room on a sigh. "Your aunt Mary writes he was shot five times in the head and several times in various other parts in his body and looks poorly even for a dead man."

The letter went on to say that the man what done it was a no-good card cheat, rat, and Evil-doer named Catfish Grimes. My uncle had just returned from a trip to California and had made his fortune. But he had not carried his fortune about with him, knowing that Tombstone was not a place to be with a big piece of money. Instead, he had hid his treasure in a safe place and had wrote down the spot on a map. He had planned to settle his affairs in Tombstone, and then he and Aunt Mary, his wife of some twenty-three years, were going to use the treasure to live the Good Life. But now an Evildoer had forced the hand of cruel fate.

"Your aunt Mary was at church, giving due praise to the Lord," Mother said, "when Uncle Ugly was waylaid in front of a place called the

Bird Cage Saloon."

When poor Uncle Ugly was brought home, Aunt Mary saw that he was not truly stone dead, and she sent for the doctor. The doctor came and did the best he could. Uncle Ugly lingered for three days before passing on to his reward.

Before he died, he put the bloody finger on Catfish Grimes and said that Grimes had done shot him and took his treasure map. The sheriff went over to where Grimes used to stay, but it was no use. The sneaky dog had flown the coop. Aunt Mary said that there was a woman who stayed at the same boarding house where Catfish stayed. Her name was Lucy Featherdip, and talk had it that she was a loose woman, a stranger to decent ways, and also sweet on Catfish. When Catfish Grimes disappeared, Lucy Featherdip disappeared too. Aunt Mary wrote that Louella Perkins, who runs the boarding house, said that Catfish Grimes was not paid up but that the Featherdip woman was.

Aunt Mary explained how grievous hurt she was, and how not a day passed since the death of her Beloved when she did not beat her breast and weep. Surely it made my heart break to read such sadness and it reduced my poor mother to a state of the shaking sobs.

Mother made a pot of fresh sassafras tea and cut me a slice of pan bread—making me know that what she had to say was Serious.

"Your aunt Mary wants you to come to Tombstone and assume the role of the Man in the family and see to it that Uncle Ugly's foul murder does not go unpunished," Mother said.

Then, with eyes glistening with tears, she read straight from the letter itself.

> *I have saved four hundred dollars in cash money, and half of it will be yours, Artemis Bonner, if you will Avenge your uncle's Cruel death.*

"You are too young to go to the Wild West," Mother said. "There are men out there who do not care for human life."

"I know this to be true, Mother Dear," I said. "But if I can bring Catfish Grimes to justice, it will be a good thing. Also, if Aunt Mary will truly give me two hundred dollars, then I will send half of it to you."

"You are such a good son," Mother said. "But I am worried about your health."

I knew my sainted mother would fear for my safety in such an adventure, but could I deny what destiny had wrought? I kissed the slender hands of Her who brought me into this world and announced that I must go. For just as there are men like Catfish Grimes in the world with no character and not enough decency to fill a thimble, so are there men like myself, of nobler stance and grander hopes, who must fight for Justice.

"Artemis," Mother said, "I see in your eyes the glint of a true Man and know you must be about man's business. I give you my blessing and wish you the best of luck. And please do not forget to send the hundred dollars."

So, with Mother's blessing and a stout lunch of cheese and fresh rolls, I boarded the train for the Untamed West.

TWO

"WHERE ARE YOU HEADED?" A young woman asked of me as the train pulled out of the station in New York. "I am headed all the way to Baltimore to visit my aunt."

"Baltimore?" said I. "That is a mere trifling! I

am headed to Arizona Territory to avenge the death of my uncle. Perhaps I shall live through it, and perhaps not. Who knows what will happen when I am out there among the gunslingers and the wild Indians?"

"Well," she said, pulling the veil across her face, "seeing that you are as brown as an Indian, I don't think you will have trouble with them."

"I believe that to be the case," I said, concealing a smile. I had no idea of what to expect from Indians, should I indeed meet them, but I have never been one to dwell on fear.

Soon I closed my eyes and fell to the blissful sleep of the innocent.

It was a long and arduous journey, and many times I longed for the comforts of my own cot or a fresh cut of tallow to ease the congestion in my chest. Nonetheless, I continued.

It took me nine and one half days to reach Tombstone, and by that time poor Uncle Ugly was in the cold ground. When Aunt Mary met me at the post office building, she was dressed all in black even down to the little pipe she smoked. She was small but stood straight as an arrow, and I could tell she was a no-nonsense woman. We said the Lord's Prayer and then went over to where my uncle was buried so I could pay my Last Respects. Uncle Ugly had been laid to rest thirty feet behind the Carlton stables with only a scratch mark in the ground to show the place.

"The tombstone will be ready tomorrow," Aunt Mary said. She spit into the corner and wiped her mouth with a delicate move of her wrist that told me she was a true lady. The tears that fell from her eyes splashed upon my heart.

"Do not worry," I said to Aunt Mary. "I will go and find Catfish Grimes and give him his just due."

"I will be obliged if you do that," she said. "And I will give you a copy of the treasure map. If you can find it, you are welcome to keep it. For with him gone I have nothing to live for."

I was surprised that there was a copy of the map. I told this to my aunt Mary, and she said that Uncle Ugly had made a copy of the map as best he could from memory while lying on his deathbed.

"He had been away for almost a whole year," Aunt Mary said. "He sent me letters from all over and told me he had a big and secret surprise for me. When he came home, he told me that the surprise was a treasure in genuine gold. He only brought home one big nugget, which he sold to buy him a pair of new boots and me a bolt of blue-striped cloth. A man with a squint eye was in the store when he bought the cloth."

"Do not tell me," I said. "The man was Catfish Grimes!"

"One and the same."

At this point Aunt Mary and me kissed and embraced in a Christian manner, and she said that she had faith in me.

She took me home and set me down to a hearty meal of mustard greens and hog jowls and buttermilk biscuits. I must say that I had my fill and then some. After the meal I looked at the map. It was a good drawn map. A red "X" marked where the treasure was.

"Where is this place?" I asked Aunt Mary.

"I do not know," she said. "Your uncle said he was not going to put that down unless he thought for sure he was going to meet his Maker, so that it would be safe."

"I guess he thought he was going to pull through," I said.

"Well, I guess that was what he thought," she said. "When I found him dead, he did have a surprised look upon his face."

I asked Aunt Mary if the map what was stolen by Catfish Grimes had the name of the place wrote on it, and she said that it did not.

"Then Catfish Grimes and me both have the same task," I said. "We must find the place where Uncle Ugly was when he discovered the treasure, and then find its location with this map."

I wrote down all the places Uncle Ugly had been, according to Aunt Mary. I would go to these places and get the treasure before Catfish Grimes got his greedy hands on it.

But first I saw to it that the tombstone was placed on the grave of my Beloved Uncle. I composed the words myself. It read like this:

Here Lies Ugly Ned Bonner
Once Alive—
Now a Goner

I looked over the list I had made and saw that Uncle Ugly had been a traveling man to the first degree. He had been not only to Tombstone but to Lincoln, New Mexico; Juarez, Mexico; Sacramento, California; Seattle, Washington; and even to Alaska. Somewhere along the way he had buried the treasure, and I was hard determined to find it.

I received but one hundred and sixty-three dollars from my aunt Mary, the other part of the money, she explained, having gone for the tombstone and a suit to bury Uncle Ugly in, which was both Proper and Fit.

"It was a store-bought suit," she said. "And hardly used."

I sent the one hundred dollars to Mother as I promised, and an extra dollar for her to give to the New York Colored Orphans Home. Having put the rest of the money in a handkerchief tied to a string around my waist, I set off for Lincoln, New Mexico, with high hopes.

THREE

LINCOLN, NEW MEXICO, was the last place Uncle Ugly had been before he came back to Tombstone. What with waiting for trains and stopping to pick up water and supplies, I could see that it was going to take me a long time to get around. But I did see my first honest-to-goodness Indians. They were riding alongside the train, looking neither to the right nor to the left, and I saw that they were carrying spears and bows and arrows. I hunkered down in my seat the best I could when I noticed one of them looking right at my window.

"We're riding over their hunting grounds." The round man sitting across from me had a big, round head, red hair, and small blue eyes that moved back and forth as if they had a mind of their own.

"They look mighty fierce to me," I said.

"You'd look fierce if they took your land, wouldn't you?" my companion said.

"I don't suppose they would attack the train?" I said.

"Naw," was the quick answer. "Every man on this train got one gun, maybe two. Besides, they don't know if there are any Buffalo soldiers on the train."

"Buffalo soldiers?"

"Yeah, Tenth Cavalry," he said. "All colored fellows like you. Excepting the officers, of course. They keep the Indians in check. You going to join up with them?"

"I'm going looking for the man who killed my uncle," I told him.

"What was your uncle's name?" the big-headed stranger asked. His hand edged closer to the handle of the gun that was in his belt.

"It was Uncle Ugly Ned Bonner."

"Oh, I didn't kill him," he said, smiling. "I ain't never killed a man named Ugly."

He took his hand away from his gun and kept on smiling. I smiled, too, but I confess it was a nervous smile.

I finally got to Albuquerque, and I found the stage that was headed through the mountains to Lincoln. The ticket master had one eye and a funny way of looking at me with it.

"You a bad man?" he asked.

"No, sir," I replied. "I am a Christian and have even taught Sunday School."

"If you know how to handle a shotgun, I will let you ride the stage to Lincoln for free," he said. "Can you do that?"

"Yes," I said, thinking that a smart fellow like me could learn to use such a weapon.

"I hope so," said the ticket master. "I truly hope so. And you'd better buy yourself a hat."

I went into a dry goods store and bought a

{13}

white hat, and I had to confess that I looked pretty good and maybe even handsome.

I was supposed to sit up on the driver's box with the shotgun on my lap and my fingers on the triggers.

"In case we get attacked by Indians or by outlaws," the driver said. He had an awful smell that made my whole body stiffen when the wind was blowing toward me.

"Have you always been a driver?" I asked, trying not to inhale.

"Used to be a barber," he said. "But I like this better. All I got to do is drive and all you got to do is shoot anybody who comes near the coach. I'm not stopping this coach until we get to the first station. That's fifteen miles. We change horses there, and then we go another fifteen miles to the second stop, then twelve miles to the third stop, and so on until we get there. If we're lucky, we'll get to Lincoln just about at sunset. If we're not there by then, we're in a world of trouble! Wipe down the brake shoes with this grease and be ready to go in fifteen minutes."

I was about to answer, but the driver had already walked away.

The ride was not a pleasant one. I spent most of my time just holding on for Dear Life. When we stopped, I got down and rubbed my sore spots and the passengers went behind a fence to take care of their needs. Then we were off again. By the time we reached Lincoln, I was sore all over and my back ached as if I had been kicked by twenty large mules.

I had been thinking about this Catfish Grimes and the fact that he had shot Uncle Ugly. I went over to a store called Murphy's and asked the counterman if he had a gun for sale.

"What kind of gun do you want?" he asked.

"That kind," I said, pointing to a weapon on the shelf behind the counter.

"That is an over and under," he said. "It is a small gun that some men carry in their boots."

"Then I will take it," I said. "And I would like to have some information as well. Have you seen a dark stranger in these parts traveling with a woman companion?"

"That I have," was the honest reply.

"And how did he call himself?" I asked.

"I cannot forget that name," the clerk said. "He called himself by the name of my favorite eating fish."

"You mean Catfish?" I said.

"That be it," he said.

I could feel my blood run cold. Catfish Grimes had the same idea I had. He was no slouch as far as the thinking department went.

"What does this Catfish fellow look like?" I asked.

"Is he a friend of yours?"

"No," I said, "he is no friend of mine."

"In that case," said the clerk, "I can tell you that he looks like a bad case. His eyes are not but a thumbnail apart and his nose is very big. I think he has led a rough life, for there is a scar on his forehead."

I thanked the clerk, paid for the over and under and a box full of bullets, and went to rent a room at the Lincoln Hotel. I would go after Catfish at the crack of dawn.

FOUR

LINCOLN, NEW MEXICO, WAS not what anybody from New York City would call a regular town. It was just a bunch of buildings squatting together near some low hills. Most of the time people sat around outside their houses and looked out over the hills to see what was coming next. Mostly what was coming next in Lincoln was trouble. I spent the next two days in Low Dives where the locals talked and played cards. Whenever I found a likely fellow, I asked of Catfish. A stoop-shouldered old man with a stream of tobacco running down his cheek said that he had seen a fellow who fit the description of Catfish and that he had had a woman with him. They had hired two Indian guides and set out toward the mountains. I asked the general direction they had gone, hired a stout fellow by the name of Charlie Bowdre to be my guide and a spindly-legged bay horse to ride upon, and set out after them the following day.

It took but a few hours to reach what Charlie called Gold Country in the hills. By then both my back and my Dignity were sorely put to the test by the rough ride, and I was reminded again that I was a City person and not used to Western ways.

Although I do believe in the Good Book and the fact that God made all living creatures, it is a mystery to me why He would make something as stupid as the lumpy, mangy, ornery, and foul-tempered beast I was riding. We traveled for two more days, and I was grateful that there were none to witness my circumstance. I was so sore, I truly wished that I had no place upon which to sit. And all the time we were trailing our dreadful prey, I was forced to listen to the heathen ramblings of my companion.

"Why don't we just forget this traveling after this here Catfish fellow and maybe rustle some cattle or steal some good horses?" he said. "I thought all you New York fellows were pretty sharp."

"Have you never heard of the Eighth Commandment?" I said. "'Thou shalt not steal'?"

"That's for honest folks," Charlie said. "It ain't for thieves."

I do not mind saying, nor do I feel shame, that many were the times I would have turned back if I had been one drop a lesser sort.

The third day that came up was hot enough to steal the ice off a dead man. It was on this day that we came upon two of the most wretched souls that I had ever laid eyes upon. They were Indians and spoke to Charlie in their lingo, which he understood. They looked upon me, and I saw not a trace of kindness in their eyes. When we had parted from them, I asked Charlie what they had said. He said that they had been hired as guides by Catfish Grimes.

"When they reached where they was going, that Catfish fella shot at them and drove them off," Charlie said. "Didn't give them as much as a Liberty dime for their troubles, either."

I put my arm around Charlie and told him that I was a True Believer and a man of my Word upon whom he could count and would not drive him off without the pay of one dollar a day that I had promised him. Charlie shook my hand warmly, and I thought the matter well settled.

That night while I slept, he slipped away like a thief in the night, taking with him all my water and the flea-bitten bay. But he had missed my money belt and the pistol I had in my boot. The words that came to my lips were not the kind that I would say before my mother, so I bit my tongue and tried my best to think Pure Thoughts.

There was nothing for me to do but to press on alone and on foot, and this I did, concerning myself with neither personal safety nor even simple comforts. I struck out boldly in a direction I hoped would be correct using Mother Wit as my guide and Courage as my staff. For nearly three hours I went on as the sun climbed higher in the sky. I tried walking in the tall grass so I would not be an easy target, but the grass was so rough it cut like a knife, so I got back onto the road. There were so many small hills that I could not see very far ahead of me, but I kept my eyes peeled for danger and my muscles ready.

I heard voices coming from just beyond a small rise. I stopped in my tracks for a while, listened carefully, then edged forward. My heart was beating fast as I wiped the sweat from my face with the back of my hand. Removing my pistol from my boot, I cocked it and peered over the rise.

The sight that came into view was amazing. Although I had never before laid eyes on the man, the beady eyes and the big nose told me at once that I had finally gained the presence of Catfish Grimes! He was a tall man with high, square shoulders and a big head that he held pushed forward.

"You can come to a halt right there," I said,

standing straight up and raising the pistol to belt level.

"And to whom do I have the honor?" His voice sounded like the barking of an old dog.

"I am Artemis Bonner, nephew of Ugly Ned Bonner, the man you shot down in cold blood in Tombstone," I said.

His upper lip curled away from his yellow teeth and his eyes narrowed. The whole right side of his face twitched as he eyed the pistol in my hand.

"And what, pray tell, brings you to this part of the world?" he asked.

"Justice!" I said simply, knowing well that the word would strike a note of fear in his evil heart.

The woman, Lucy Featherdip, of course, was with him. She was a passing comely woman with a gentle face no doubt meant for better things than the wayward life of the Depraved. She cowered behind Catfish's back as I approached them, and I felt it a pity that it was I who caused her to tremble. I bade Catfish Grimes to kneel and to put his hands behind his back. This he did, all the while peering at my

{21}

pistol and muttering the vilest of oaths beneath his breath. The Featherdip woman stood the whole time in complete silence, watching me. I took a rope from Catfish's belt and tied his hands as tightly as I could, not caring a whit for his comfort.

"Will you be tying me, too?" Lucy Featherdip asked. She had a sweet voice but lower than most women back East.

"No, ma'am," I replied, putting my pistol into my belt. "Rest assured that I know the part of a gentleman as well as any man."

At first, I thought she was choking back the tears, moved by my gentle manners. Then I thought she might be ill. She was making what seemed to be choking noises from deep in her throat. Then, without warning, and in a manner not becoming one of her sex, she spat into my eyes, blinding me for the moment.

To tell the truth—and there is nothing to tell if it is not the truth—I was made furious by this unladylike behavior. And when, through my blurred vision, I saw her close the distance between us, I had already decided that she did not deserve the role of gentleman I had elected to play for her.

I did not, in all honesty, see the first blow coming. I felt it instead, and went backward onto the ground. I came quickly to my feet, although my head had not cleared. She swung again, and although I lifted my arm in my defense, the second blow landed as heavily as the first. Lucy Featherdip could hit like a blue mule could kick. Each time she swung, I fell anew. Nor, possessed by the Devil's own strength, did she tire. My pistol had fallen from my belt, and I was at her mercy. I was soon completely baffled by her blows and lay dazed upon the ground, ears ringing, in perfect disgrace.

Moments later, Grimes was up and about, untied by the Featherdip woman.

"Poor dear," she said to Grimes. Then, as he looked at me as if I were something the cat dragged in, she delivered me another blow from her right hand, which put me into an unconscious state.

FIVE

WHEN I AWOKE, IT WAS TO THE splashing of water in my face. For a happy moment I thought my rescue was at hand, but this was far from the truth.

"Where is the treasure?" Catfish Grimes stared me in the eyes. His breath smelled like fresh sheep droppings, and at that close distance I could see that his complexion was no improvement over putrid mutton.

"I do not know the whereabouts of the treasure," I said, "but at any rate I would sooner die than to tell the likes of you. For you are a vile man who is not acquainted with either Decency or Goodness."

"Yes, that is so," he said, and then he laughed so dark a laugh that the Devil himself must have shuddered. "And since you have spoken the truth, I will do likewise and say that I would rather kill you than talk with you." And with this he lifted his own pistol toward me.

"Oh, do not kill him now," said Lucy Featherdip, "for I am a soft-hearted woman and cannot stand to see a man die, even if he is as homely as this one."

This hurt me to my very heart, for I have always thought of myself as a favorite with women, although still lacking in experience in matters of True Love.

"We ought to shoot him in the nose." Catfish

pushed his face close to mine. "To remind him of how nosy he is."

The Featherdip woman said that there was no need to kill me, that they could just tie me up and leave me, and that the coyotes would probably eat me.

"They will eat anything if they get hungry enough," she said.

Catfish replied that this would do well and told me to take my hat off and thank the lady for sparing my wretched life.

I removed my hat, about to say a halfhearted "Thank you, ma'am," when Catfish Grimes, the dirty sneak-rat, cold conked me from behind.

I do not know how long I lay stupefied, but when I woke, it was to a hurting head and deep misery. But even this did not stop me from keeping my Senses about me. I opened one eye slowly and saw something tall in front of me. I reckoned it was Catfish, so I closed my eyes again. After a long time I opened my eyes again, just a mite this time, and saw that the moon was high in the sky above me. In front of me was the tallest cactus plant I had ever seen. My ankles were tied together around the cactus, and my wrists were tied in front of me. I started to get up on one elbow when I felt a terrible pain in my head and another pain in my leg.

The pain in my head was from the whomping that Catfish had laid on me, and the pain in my leg was from the needles in the cactus. Any way I moved, that cactus stuck in me and in the most terrible places.

I heard a howling off to one side, and I looked over and saw two coyotes sitting on a ridge. My blood ran cold, for I did not wish to be a midnight snack for anything that looked like a dog and was not Civilized.

The rope that held my wrists was not very thick, but it stunk something terrible and left a bad taste in my mouth as I started chewing on it. To tell the Truth, I did not enjoy chewing on that rope, but knew I had to get through it before them coyotes figured out that they could come and chew on me.

When I got my wrists free, I sat up and looked face to face with that cactus. I tried wriggling around a little, but every time I did, I got stuck in the private parts. I thought about Catfish riding away and thinking about me and wondered if he had a smile on his evil face.

"Yip! Yip! Yip! Oooo yip!"

That's how the coyote sounded. I turned and saw that one of them had edged a little closer to me. The cactus was as tall as a man, and almost as big around. Every time I tried to reach around it, I got stuck. I tried to pull it down toward me, but all I got was needles in my ankles. They stuck in me and they burned something terrible.

I thought about trying to eat my way through it, but I did not want to get a cactus needle in the lips, so I gave that up real quick.

"Yip! Yip! Yip! Oooo yip!"

That coyote was getting closer.

"Get away!" I called to the beast in a sharp voice, but he didn't seem to mind that much. He just turned his head to one side and gave me a good looking over.

The cactus was full of needles, and it was tall, but it was not that strong looking.

The second coyote moved a little closer and I could see that both of them were in need of a good meal, which I hoped would not be me.

I do not know how it feels to be eaten, but I knew that I did not wish to spend the last minutes of my life being chewed on. I took a deep breath and put my hands around that cactus plant and began to pull myself up. It was the worst hurt I ever had in my whole life. The first time I got halfway up, I fell backward and landed hard on my head. One of them coyotes moved a little closer.

"Yip! Yip! Yip! Oooo yip!"

I grabbed that cactus for all I was worth and pulled myself up. With my ankles tied on the other side, I had to lie on it just to get up, and the needles stuck in every place I had. When I got all the way up, I threw myself against that cactus with everything I had. It bent over and then came straight back. I threw myself at it again. It went over and came back.

The third time, the cactus broke off, and me and it rolled over two or three times before we stopped. I got my legs from around it and pushed it off of me, and I do believe that those needles coming out of me was every bit as nasty as when they came in.

I untied my ankles and threw the ropes at the coyotes, who slunk off as soon as I stood up. The wind picked up and blew sand and dirt in my face, but I did not care. I looked about and saw a small hill, up which I quickly climbed. From there I could see Lincoln in the distance and knew that it was a long way to walk and my feet were already sore. Every little piece of me was hurting, but I had no choice but to walk back to town or to give up my Mission. All the way back I picked out cactus needles from places I could reach easily and walked with my legs apart so I wouldn't aggravate the other places too much.

SIX

IN LINCOLN I BOUGHT ANOTHER pistol from Murphy's, resolved to be more careful with this one than I had been with the last. I was feeling poorly but did not offer that as an excuse to myself or to the World. I knew well what my business had to be and was determined to be about that business.

I had learned that Catfish Grimes was not an easy sort to deal with, nor would the Featherdip woman be a Pushover. But they would learn that Artemis Bonner knew more than what lay between the pages of his Hymnal and would not tolerate being taken lightly.

I went to the stage office, which was also the sheriff's office and the post office. A young boy was sitting in one corner chewing on a piece of stick, and a pinch-faced deputy was reading a newspaper. I found out from the deputy that a couple fitting the description of Catfish and Lucy had booked passage that very morning.

"And were they in good humor?" I asked.

"No, they were not," came the swift reply. "They looked like a couple of horses that had been run all night and put away wet."

"To what city are they headed?" I asked.

"That's none of your business, boy," the deputy answered.

"Sir, you have before you a Determined Man," I said. "I do not wish to do you harm, but it is only fair to warn you that I am from New York City, have a steady aim, and have also been known to be of quick temper."

"You're not Billy the Kid, are you?" he asked, his eyes wide with fear.

"You may call me what you will," I said. "Just give me the information I need."

"They are headed for Juarez City, Mexico," he said directly.

I thanked him for that information and asked him when the next coach left for Juarez City.

"There ain't none," he said, looking back to his paper.

That was not a good answer for my purpose, and I sat down on the curb outside the barber shop and put my head in my hands. I did not know what to do.

"You going to Juarez City?" a small voice kind of chirped at me from behind.

I opened my eyes and looked up to see the same boy I had seen in the deputy's office.

"That is my destination," I said.

"That's where I'm going, too," the boy said. He was a handsome youth, with dark eyes, dark hair that came out from under a big floppy hat, and a little smile that went up one side of his face more than it went up the other side. He leaned against a hitching post and looked down at me.

"How are you going to get to Juarez City?" I asked.

"Got to hitch me a ride," he said. "They ain't no regular coach to Juarez. Only reason most people go down there is keep from getting hanged. You scared of getting hanged?"

"I am not an outlaw," I said. "I am trying to find the man who killed my uncle."

"I'm an Indian, you know," he said. "I can find most anybody."

To be sure, he looked to be of the white persuasion, and of the poor white persuasion at that. I leaned back a little to take a good look at him, and he leaned back a little and straightened up so I could take my look.

"What is your name?" I asked.

"Laughing Bear is my Indian name," he said. "And my other name is Frolic Brown. You can call me Frolic if you want."

"How old are you, Frolic?" I asked.

"Almost thirteen," he said.

"Surely you must have a family here that would worry about you if you traveled away with a stranger."

"Nope. I ain't even from around here." Frolic looked down and shook his head. Then he sat down next to me on the curb. "I'm from back East. We lived in Delaware for a while, but when my mom died, me and my father moved to Lancaster, Pennsylvania. He was working in the mines there. My mom was Cherokee."

I did not want to ask the whereabouts of his father but felt duty-bound to do so, and so I did.

"Is your father here in Lincoln?" I asked.

"Nope. Got blowed up in the mines," Frolic said. "So I come out here looking to be a cowboy, but I ain't found a job yet."

"Well, you cannot come with me," I said. "I am looking to avenge the death of my uncle, Ugly Ned Bonner, and might have to conduct myself in a violent manner. I am not a man who would be good company for an orphan."

"Why you going to Juarez?" Frolic lowered his voice and edged over close to me.

"That's where Catfish Grimes is headed," I said.

"He the one who shot up your uncle?"

"Yes," I said. "And I am looking for him and Lucy Featherdip, who is his friend."

"Lucy who?"

"Lucy Featherdip," I said. "The hardest-hitting woman I have ever heard about."

"They's two of them"—Frolic stretched out his fingers—"and only one of you?"

"You can't come with me, Frolic," I said. "It is too dangerous."

"I can track down a man that's buried six feet deep," he said. "If a man tries to get away from me, he don't stand even a bit of a chance."

Now Frolic Brown kept on about how he

could help me track down Catfish because he was part Cherokee. But to me he was a mere child who had a Lot to Learn. Still, he had an honest face, and a friendly one at that, and I did not mind having someone to pass the time of day with as I did the tracking.

"What's your name?"

"Artemis Bonner."

"Artemis Bonner, I'm going to find him for you!"

I looked into Frolic's eyes and saw that he was stone serious. He was also right that one Catfish Grimes and one Lucy Featherdip added up to two, while I added up to only one. I told Frolic that I might take him with me but not to get too close to me in case there was any gunplay.

"Nobody better mess with you and me," Frolic said.

His voice had the ring of Pure D. Truth in it, and I was happy to hear it.

It was six days before we found a couple of fellows who were headed for Juarez, and six long days at that, but when they left, Artemis Bonner and Frolic were with them. But it was not the same Artemis Bonner who had left

New York City after kissing his Dear Mother farewell. For Catfish Grimes had nearly sent my soul to its Heavenly Home and had revealed himself to be through-and-through Mean. Thus is was that when I looked into my mirror, I saw looking back at me a hardened Man. And when I looked by my side I saw a boy of twelve, but a boy who was an orphan and an Indian, and a Cherokee to boot.

SEVEN

WHEN ME AND FROLIC REACHED Juarez, we knew at once that it was an Awful place. Whatever piece of you that the heat did not kill off was left to the flies. The flies would light upon anything that moved and would not quit for love nor money.

"You want some licorice?" Frolic asked.

"You got some?" I asked.

Frolic carried a leather pouch with him and commenced to dig down in it. Then he pulled out a little tin marked Tutt's Pills. He opened it and I saw it was filled with licorice candy.

"They come all the way from a store in Gettysburg," he said.

"Lots of Cherokees eat licorice?" I asked, taking two pieces to be sociable.

"Some do," he said.

He looked at me with a shamed face, but then he saw that I was smiling and he smiled back.

"Cherokees do a lot of different things," he said.

"Well, let us see that they keep a sharp eye out for danger," I said, "and do not spend their time thinking about licorice."

I could see that Frolic did not like those hard words at all. But I knew that I could not give in to childish things if I was to succeed on my Mission.

The first thing we noticed in Juarez was that all of the Natives spoke Spanish, and I have never heard so much foreign talk in all my Born Days. There were a lot of people from America there, too, and they were a mangy lot, given to Strong Drink and making sport with the local women.

We found a little room over a *Cantina*, and I could not sleep either day or night for all the noise. When people were not playing guitars or stamping around with what they called dancing, they were having gunfights. The first night, a bullet came right through the floor and through my slop jar. I will not even say what a mess it made. Frolic slept like a newborn baby and was not much for company.

The next morning we went downstairs and bought us a plate of beans and rice.

"I asked the man dishing out the beans about Catfish Grimes and Lucy Featherdip, but either he did not know where they were or he was being close lipped about it," I told Frolic.

"I could look into his eyes and see if he is telling the truth," Frolic said. "That's what Cherokees do sometimes."

"You saw that?" I asked him.

"Sort of," he said.

"Did you *really* live with the Cherokees?" I asked.

"I told you, my mother was a Cherokee!" he said. When he got mad, his lips stuck out so he looked like he was sucking on a lemon.

I figured I would let the subject of him looking into people's eyes to see if they were telling the truth rest for a while, and anyway, I was not feeling the best. My stomach was growling and rumbling, and I came down with a pain that moved around just enough to make me feel miserable.

Me and Frolic took the map over to what looked like a City Hall and showed it to one of the fellows sitting behind a desk. A soldier stood near the desk, and he gave me and Frolic each a hard look and we returned the same to him.

"This is the spot that my poor uncle is buried," I said, not wanting to reveal that it was a Treasure map.

The Mexican official put the map down on the desk in front of him, looked at it, and then looked up at me. Then he called over another fellow and they looked at the map together.

"You a gringo?" the second fellow asked.

I had never been called a gringo before, and I did not like it the first time.

"I am from New York City," I said.

"How do you know this is where your uncle is buried?" the first fellow asked.

"That is an easy question," I said, crossing my fingers under the desk so that I would not be cursed for All Eternity for lying. "That is a peaceful place that my uncle saw one day and said that he wanted to be buried there."

They spoke between them for a minute in

their own lingo and then one of them nodded.

"Come with me," he said.

He took me to the front door and pointed toward some mountains that lay off in the distance.

I looked at the map. There were some triangles on it that could have been mountains. "Thank you, my good man," I said.

He nodded at me and looked me up and down carefully, and I let him take a good look before I left.

"How come Catfish give you a map to show where he is?" Frolic asked.

I had not told Frolic about the Treasure, and was not sure that I wanted to. But I know that Blessings come to those who Trust and decided to bare my soul to the little Cherokee.

"It is my uncle's Treasure map," I said. "Catfish Grimes also has a copy, and we must find the treasure before he does."

"You got a treasure, and you got a Catfish Grimes." Frolic nodded slowly. "That's a good life."

What he meant was that it was an Exciting life, which was the Truth.

The cowboys in Juarez were mostly scalawags and worse, but they had horses, and I brought a gray nag who had seen Better Days. The saddlebags that came with the nag had three bullet holes in them, and I asked where they might have come from.

"A horse thief from Wyoming Territory put them holes in there," the cowboy said.

His words were easy to understand, but I did not hear the Ring of Truth in them. Still, I was inclined to buy the horse, for it was better than walking.

I got on first and tried to get Frolic up, but every time I gave him a pull, I slid down. Some cowboys were standing near the side of the stable, and they commenced to laugh. Finally I pushed Frolic up on the horse and then went around to the other side to get up myself. I hadn't a bit more grabbed that horse by the saddle than he took off running, making me hold on for Dear Life. It took Frolic near a mile to bring him to a stop. The next time I tried to get up on him, I went around on the same side that Frolic got on.

"Which way do we have to go?" I asked Frolic.

"I don't know," Frolic said.

"Can't you track them down?" I said, remembering that he was a Cherokee.

"I got to see a man first before I can track him down like a dog," Frolic said.

Well, that made sense, and we started off.

EIGHT

THE TREK TOWARD THE mountains did not look like much, but the better part of a day passed and we did not seem to be getting any closer. I did not know much about Mexicans, and when I passed them on the road, I did not know how to take the hard looks of their men. We did not stop and try to chat with none of them, and they did not pay us much mind either, so I thought I would leave well enough alone.

Frolic seemed to like riding, but I was getting pretty sore, so I pulled off into a little stand of trees that looked a little like willows in order to stretch out. I tied the horse to a bush and eased on down into the grass, and it felt as good as if it had been a feather bed. We had bought a tin of beans, and Frolic had just sat himself on a flat rock and started to open them when we heard the sound of another horse whinnying nearby.

"You want me to take a look?" Frolic asked.

"Don't much care," I said.

Frolic went up to a rise and peeked over it. "A woman's fixing up a saddle on a horse," Frolic said. "Looks better than the horse we got."

"Probably a donkey," I said. "The Mexicans have a lot of donkeys."

"Nope." Frolic shielded his eyes from the sun. "She's a black woman and she's pretty big."

I looked over to where Frolic was looking and saw that we were near a little house and a woman was just cinching down a saddle on the horse. At first it did not make a bit of difference to me, but then I saw that woman throw a leg over the horse's back and start galloping away toward Juarez.

"That's Lucy Featherdip!" I said in a hoarse whisper. We watched her going away, riding astraddle like a man.

I stood up and crossed the road and looked in the direction she had come from. It was a small, beat-up-looking place with a grass roof.

"They must just be leaving," I said.

"They got some smoke coming out of the chimney," Frolic noticed.

I looked and saw the thin wisp of smoke, and I could feel my blood begin to heat up.

I waited a bit more after Lucy rode off, and then, after telling Frolic to stay behind me, I took out my pistol and started up the road. When I got within a stone's throw, I could see that the place was like a lean-to, made of sticks and grass.

"You going to shoot the gun?" Frolic whispered.

"I might. But first I got to be sure Catfish is inside that house," I said. "I could set fire to the whole thing, but I know in my heart that it would not be Christian to burn up a stranger."

"Here come somebody now," Frolic said.

I ducked down as quick as I could and caught my breath, for I had just received a big Surprise and the Shock of my Life. For Catfish Grimes himself came out of that little place and he was as naked as a jay bird.

"Keep your head down!" I whispered to Frolic.

"It's down!" he said.

I looked over at him, and he had his head

down on the ground with his arms over it. He did not look a whole lot like my idea of a Cherokee.

Catfish Grimes went over to one side of the shack, picked up a shovel, and started scooping out a hole in the ground. Now he had his back to me. And although I Hated Catfish through and through and would be hard pressed even to offer him the Right Hand of Fellowship, I did not want to be a dirty coward and shoot him in the back. But I did not want him to turn around and cause me any undue trouble, naked as he was, as I was not sure I had regained all of my strength from my long journey and my stomach pains.

I looked around and saw a stout stick, and I picked it up as quiet as you please. By the time I had done this, Catfish had set himself squat over the hole he had scooped out. I ran over to him as fast as I could with the stick over my head. He heard me coming and started to turn around, but it was too late.

Whomp! Whomp! I hit him two good shots alongside of his head, and he rolled over onto the grass.

Whomp! I hit him again.

"Take that, you thieving son of a cross-eyed buzzard!" I said, not caring how he would feel about the Insult.

I continued to whomp him until he fell out half dead. I did not want to kill him right then, but to make him pay for the misdeeds he had done to me and Uncle Ugly and to see him Repent on his knees.

Frolic run up and gave Catfish a kick on the leg.

"Look around for a rope to tie him with," I said.

Frolic found a small piece of rope from a horse Catfish had tied in back of the hut he and Lucy lived in, and he tied his hands good. Then me and Frolic sat ourselves down to think on how we could torture him. As I remembered being tied to that cactus outside of Lincoln, New Mexico, I do not like to admit that there was not a kind thought that entered my head, but that was the true and only Case.

"He is really ugly," Frolic said. "Mean-looking, too."

"Where were you when I was out here whomping him?" I asked.

"Looking out for that woman," Frolic said, as

Catfish began to groan and move around.

"Do not move too much," I said, "or I will be forced to whomp you again."

Then I saw a long line of red ants moving slowly along past a berry bush, and I knew I had the answer to what to do with Catfish.

I traced the ants back about ten yards or so until I came to their hill. Then I started digging a six-foot hole right as I told Frolic what I was going to do to Catfish. I told him nice and loud so that Catfish would hear every word.

"Artemis Bonner!" Catfish was so mad he was growling like a bear, and the sound of his Evil voice made Frolic back off. "You are as evil as your uncle was ugly, and I wish I had shot you an even dozen times and one extra time right through the heart for good luck."

"Well, you had your chance, Catfish," I said. "But now is my time."

When the hole was done, I got Frolic to help me drag Catfish over to the hole and me and him lowered Catfish Grimes into it, standing him upright until only his foul head stuck out. I packed the dirt around him good and went into the cabin. By the time I had found some honey and come back out, he was cussing and spitting at Frolic and Frolic was trying to throw dust in his beady eyes.

"Please do not do this awful thing to me," Catfish said. "Let me go and we can split the treasure between us."

"I would rather play bid whist with the Devil himself than to make a deal with the likes of you, Catfish Grimes," I said, amazed that someone of such a low position would imagine that a decent man like me would deal with him.

Hc closed his eyes as I smeared the honey all over his big nose. It did not take but a minute before the first of the ants had made its way over to him. He watched it coming and was as helpless as a newborn babe.

"Ha-haaa!" I laughed out loud so that Catfish was sure to hear me and suffer the humiliation. He looked at me and then down at the ants.

"He's the meanest-looking man I ever did see in all my life," Frolic said. Then he walked toward the little grass hut.

"Who's the kid?" Catfish growled. His eyes were going back and forth between the ants and Frolic.

"He is my partner and Friend to boot," I said,

pushing my face near his so he could see the Satisfaction I had. "And now I will leave you to your Fate."

Frolic took whatever he could find in the cabin, which I did not mind because I felt they were our due Reward for all the trouble we had been put through. Then we started back toward our horse.

"You want to take his horse?" Frolic asked.

"You are a child," I said, realizing that I must be the example to this mere youth, "and do not understand the nature of Moral Living. We cannot sink to becoming horse thieves, and that is that."

NINE

AS WE RODE AWAY, I HUMMED a ditty I had heard in a theater on Thirteenth Street and Third Avenue in New York City and was soon taken with the pleasure of the moment. Among the things that we had taken from Catfish's miserable little cabin was a spyglass, one of the brass kind they use on ships, and when we had rode about the distance of a half mile, I turned and looked at

Catfish through the glass.

Much to my surprise I found that I had made a mistake. His big nose was covered with red ants, but he was eating most of them faster than they could eat him. He did not have a beard but he did have a good three days' stubble on his weak chin. When the ants had made their way through the stubble and were climbing over his lips to get at the honey on his nose, he would open his mouth. Half of the little devils would just crawl in, and the ones that got past he was licking at with his tongue.

"Look at that!" I said, handing the spyglass to Frolic.

"He's licking up them ants like they was made out of maple syrup," Frolic said.

And that was truly the case. I had seen some horrible things in my day, and some things that even the most charitable person would call vile if they had to put a name to it. But I had never seen anything so disgusting as a grown man of the Human Species licking red ants off his face and eating them. What I had long suspected was now revealed to me as Truth: Catfish Grimes was the lowest, foulest, most bat-brained, loathsome, skunk-sucking dog that had ever been born.

I started off to ride back to the cabin, having in mind to whomp his head right off his body. Then, off to the right, I seen the Featherdip woman riding up. Now I figured I owed her a little something and was glad she was dropping by for the merrymakings. When she saw me, she brought her bay to a stop and pulled out a pistol. I knew she could punch, but I never saw a woman who could hit more than the broad side of a wall standing six inches from it with a pistol.

"Duck down behind me, Frolic," I said as I took out my own pistol, the one I had bought at Murphy's. It was an A. J. Aubrey and a pretty piece of machinery, too. I raised it above my head so that she could see it plain. This she did.

"Do not depend on my gentle manners," I called to her. "For since our last meeting I have cast them aside. You see before you a man who longs for what is Right and who is determined to bring Justice to you and Catfish Grimes. Surrender yourself or I will Shoot to Kill!"

Her first shot hit the handle of the A. J. Aubrey and sent it spinning in the air. The next shot came hard on the heels of the first, and I felt a hard burning at the side of my head. Naturally my hand went to that place. What I felt was a strange shape to my ear and the flow of Blood. I knew that she had come to within no less than a whisker of ending my life. I wheeled the horse I was riding and gave him my heels and slapped him in the withers at the same time. With Frolic hanging on behind me, I hightailed it until I did not hear any more bullets whistling about my head. When I finally stopped and looked back through the spyglass, I could see Lucy Featherdip digging Catfish out of the ground. And it was with a broken heart that I watched this and then the two of them kissing and carrying on like the uncultured heathens they were.

TEN

WHEN WE GOT BACK TO THE *Cantina*, I got some whiskey and poured a little on my hurt ear and did also inspect it closely in the looking glass. Needless to say, I was sorry to see its poor condition.

"Well, she's sure lucky she shot you and not me," Frolic said. "You don't shoot a Cherokee and get away with it. I'd of went right at her and—"

"Frolic," I said, calming my nerves the best I could, "shut up before I see to it you do not ever see thirteen."

It was my Firm Belief that every man should do three things before he passed on to Glory. One was to make peace with his Maker; the second was to get a bank account so that he would be Established; and the third was to live until his twenty-first birthday. I had got but only partway through the list, not having either a bank account and being far from twenty-one. I was also being sorely used in the patience department. Although I have always had an even Temper and the habit of keeping a cool head, I decided to buy another pistol and go out after Catfish and Lucy again and shoot it out to the Bloody Death, and I told Frolic the same.

"If you want to leave—well, now is your chance," I told the boy.

"You need me," he said. "I can't leave now."

We went to a saloon called *El Veneno Real* and asked there if anyone had a gun for sale.

"Did a wee mousey chew your ear off?" a tall red-headed fellow with eyes like china saucers said, meaning to belittle me.

I told him that I cut the ear shaving, meaning to keep my Business to myself, and spat on the floor. Me and Frolic then sat in the corner having tea and feeling a bit glum. I had mine with sugar and he had his straight. Another fellow—he said he was an Irishman—came to me and said that a big-nosed fellow was on the other side of town trying to sell a gun, and that maybe I could go buy it cheap because the fellow looked hard up.

"Is that all the conversation he had?" I asked.

"No, there was a woman with him and they were wanting to know the best way to get to Sacramento, California," the Irishman said, "and the man was searching for some salve to put on his nose."

None other, I said to myself, than Catfish Grimes! He had not found the treasure after all. But I had no gun, and Catfish and Lucy had at least two.

"What do you think we're going to do?" Frolic asked.

"They are still searching for my uncle's treasure," I said. "And they are going to Sacramento to look for it. We will go there as well."

I have always been known as a Bright Fellow and realized that I must use my Quick and Agile mind in this adventure. No more Daniel would I be, walking into the lion's den created by Catfish and Lucy! I would instead create my own trap. (Although in my secret Heart I often gave a rousing cheer for Daniel's Holy Ways and his true grit.)

So it was that I let it be known that I was leaving at once for Sacramento, the next place on my uncle's journey, and that I was in a good frame of Mind.

Me and Frolic were running out of money, so we sold Catfish's spyglass, a vanity mirror that must have belonged to Lucy Featherdip, and our horse. All of that did not get us that much money, but we also found a job as cook and water boy for a wagon train headed toward California.

There are things in life that I do not like to do and things in life that I hate to do. Working as a cook on a wagon train was terrible. The wagon master made me sit in the last wagon, which was nothing more than a buckboard. Frolic and I took turns trying to keep the fire under the beans going and keeping the beans from slopping over into the wagon. I tried to cut off a piece of the meat to see how it tasted, but it was too tough to cut. I told this to the wagon master when he looked in on us.

"It was too tough to cut yesterday, too," he said. "But by this time tomorrow it's gonna be just about right."

Frolic did not fare any better, being threatened to be shot four times and being kicked twice.

It was hard work, but I began to realize something of my true and actual Nature that I had not wanted to face. It was that beneath my calm and handsome face, a face that belonged in the alto section of the Choir rather than in the rough trails and deserts of the Untamed West, there was a crafty and shrewd brain that was capable of cunning and, yes, *even being Devious*. As the wagon train made its way to Sacramento, I tried hard to balance the man I had become with the training I had received in the meetings I had attended at the Temperance Union.

When the train stopped in the mountains to repair a busted axle, I took the time to write a letter to my Beloved Mother, telling her of my deep thoughts and begging her not to worry about her Darling Son.

ELEVEN

WE REACHED SACRAMENTO in the late afternoon, and it was hot as blazes. The countryside around the town was just about as nice as you would want it, but there wasn't much to Sacramento itself.

"Do it get this hot in New York City?" Frolic asked me.

We had left the wagon train at a ranch a mile or so outside of the city and were walking the rest of the way. Frolic's clothes were soaked through, and his hair was plastered to his face. He looked up at me and I thought I saw a look of pure misery, but he stuck out his lower lip, the way he did sometimes, and kept going on.

"It gets hotter than this in New York," I said. "But when it does, all you have to do is go inside one of the tall buildings and stand under a fan."

"Wouldn't get me in them buildings," he said.

"Need to rest awhile?" I asked.

"No," he said, looking down.

The town itself looked like it didn't want to do nothing but sit in the hills and mind its own business. Part of it looked like it might have been Mexican, with a church and some low buildings with either white or pink walls, and red roofs. The white buildings gleamed in the bright sunlight. Off to one side was another part of town, and that looked a little like Juarez but had the same kind of clapboard buildings I had seen in Tombstone.

We headed toward the low buildings and found a hotel near the Central Pacific Railroad. It did not look too fancy on the outside, and the inside was not much of an improvement.

"It's fifty cents a night if you want a room all to yourself and twenty-five cents if you ain't that particular," the clerk said.

Me and Frolic were particular, but we decided to Rough It. We got into a room with a skinny-lipped fellow from Boston, and I gave him a warm handshake even though I was not partial to Strangers.

"And why have you young gentlemen come all the way out to California?" he asked after we told him where we were from.

"For the Adventure," I told him. "And why are you in California?"

"I am an artist and I am going to look for some Indians to paint," he said.

Now that was a Tom-Fool answer if I ever heard one, and I sat on it for a while. Then I asked him why on earth he had come all the way to California when he could have had all the Indians he wanted to draw up in New York or maybe Pennsylvania. I was sorry I asked that, because he talked for nigh onto an hour telling me how there were different kinds of Indians.

"As a matter of fact," he said, "Mr. Frolic here looks somewhat like an Indian."

"It ain't no *Mr.* Frolic," Frolic said. He was lying on the far side of the bed. "The name is Frolic D. Brown, and I'm a Cherokee."

The man from Boston went on talking about how wonderful it was to see a real Cherokee, and finally I asked him if he did not mind shutting up his face and he looked hurt. People from Boston must be touchy.

Frolic pulled the cover over him and soon slept the good sleep of the Innocent. I settled between him and the man from Boston and I was glad he was as skinny as he was. He also took off his stockings, rolled them up, and put them into his boots. Probably another thing they are fond of in Boston.

I knew Catfish would be looking for the treasure as soon as he could, so the first thing in the morning, I got Frolic up and started out.

"What does the D stand for in your name?" I asked him as we went over to the Union Hotel.

"Don't stand for nothin'," he said. "It's just something I tell grown-ups."

That was good thinking and I knew that Frolic was pushing on to young manhood.

The Union Hotel was as swell a place as any-body had a right to be in, and when the man behind the desk came over to see what we wanted, I thought he looked pretty swell, too. I inquired if he had ever heard of my uncle.

"We don't have many Black fellows in here," he said. "And if they come in, they're just pass-ing through. I wouldn't remember him."

"He has made his Fortune in gold," I said. "And it does not matter what Color he is."

"If he had a claim around here, he would have to file it," he said. "Go over there and see if there's one listed." He pointed across the street.

We went to the Claim and Assaying office and asked if there was a claim filed for my uncle. The clerk wrote down his name in a neat hand and looked it up in a big book.

"A fellow named Bonner staked a small claim out about nine miles or so past Sutter's Fort, but that was nearly five years ago. It wasn't renewed and I don't have any record of assaying any gold from the area."

My heart was filling up my chest as I left the office. It was like a Bonner not to reveal the True Nature of his fortune. I had taken a good look at the location of the claim on the map, and I decided to set out for it that very afternoon, letting no grass grow under my feet.

Frolic and me stopped at a restaurant and got some eggs and grits with a strick-o-lean apiece and felt a lot better than we had the day before.

"Why do you think that artist from Boston did not want to draw me?" Frolic asked me.

"Well, I do not know the answer to that, unless it is because you are not full-blooded the way some Indians are," I said.

Frolic looked up from his plate, then leaned back and squinted his eyes like he was trying to

figure out if it was really me that had pro-
nounced those words.

"You can never tell what blood a Cherokee
has," he said.

"I guess that is true," I answered, and went
back to cleaning up my plate.

TWELVE

AFTER FILLING OUR
bellies, we rented a mule and started off. Uncle
Ugly had made a claim just a few miles away
from a creek bed, and it took us most of the day
to find the place that I thought was the right
one. I must confess that Frolic was not much
help.

There was a small path that led from the
creek bed into the woods, which were not too
thick.

"It should be just about around here," I said.

Frolic got down off the mule and started
looking around.

"Somebody done been here," he said. "They
left some of their stuff."

Sure enough, he had found a chewed-up
pipe and a small sack of tobacco. We opened it

up and saw that the tobacco was molded through.

"What are we going to do now?" Frolic asked.

"I don't rightly know that," I answered. "But I do know the Good Lord does not want me to rest tonight on the bare ground out here in the woods. We got to build a lean-to."

Frolic went for that in a big way, and soon we had gathered enough sticks and branches to build us something nice.

"If I was back in Lancaster, I would be selling the *Lancaster Intelligencer* or carrying coal to people's houses. You can make good money if you carry fast," Frolic said. "You ever get to Lancaster, you just look up Coho and Wiley and tell them you know me."

I thought about being back in New York City and Swell Timing over on Third Avenue with the stevedores and the girls from Mulberry Street. Those times were past, though, and I knew I was a grown man and had to put away Foolish Things.

I had forgot to buy cheese and had only some hard rolls, a stick of licorice, and a tin of Colburn's mustard that I had taken from the wagon train. Around Sacramento it was warm in the day but cold at night, and I wished that Frolic and I had bought some blankets. I was tired and hungry and longing for the Soft Life of pillows and Indoor Plumbing. But I did not dwell on these thoughts for long, for I had grown used to Adversity and Hard Luck. Also, I knew that Frolic was watching me, me being his Ideal, and that I must carry myself well for his sake.

We spent several days in our little camp, and I could tell that Frolic was growing fond of it. Even Catfish Grimes got out of my mind for a while as we lived as Children of Nature. It came to me that I could not place anything in the area that looked like the drawing on the treasure map, but I decided not to worry about it none but relax and refresh my mind. As it was, I almost refreshed myself into an early grave. It is truly said that when the living gets too easy, there is a notion to forget that Life is a Vale of Sorrow and full of Trials and Tribulations.

One evening I had made a little fire and was heating up a piece of fat I had bought from a man who traveled the area with a brace of horses and a wagon made out to look like the old Conestoga kind. I figured to heat up the skillet and grease it down and then go to the creek and fish for our supper. As Providence would have it, I caught a fish, unhooked him, and gave him to Frolic to clean.

"We get tired of fish, I can kill us a bear," Frolic said.

Frolic went on about how he would trap the bear, and I listened to him real close and tried to figure out whether he was bragging on himself or not. Then we plunked that fish down in the pan, fried him up smartly, and ate him. Eating a goodly fried fish in the woods is as satisfying a thing as a man can do, and in a little while we were both sitting down feeling pleased with ourselves. I stretched out in the lean-to we had built, and Frolic went down to the creek to wash his feet, which was good, because Cleanliness is next to Godliness, and if I had had my boots off I would have done the same.

But I had given up Vigilance and had let my Watchful Eye fall asleep. Because just then I heard a clicking sound behind me and turned around to find myself staring into the biggest gun I had ever before seen.

"You reckon this is as good a place for you to

die as any?" Catfish Grimes was squinting down the barrel of the pistol.

"I reckon it is," I said, resigned to Unfortunate Fate. "Are you going to give me a chance to make my Peace with the Almighty?"

"We are not the ones to beg Mercy of," came a voice from my left side. It was Lucy Featherdip. "We could have killed you in your sleep last night, Artemis Bonner, but it would be too peaceful a way for you to die after the miseries you have caused us. For doing what you done the last time we laid eyes on your miserable form, I must admit, and Catfish agrees, that you are a filthy, lice-infested, ferret-faced, slew-footed, foul-smelling baboon and a No-Good Rat as well."

They were rough words heaped upon my head, especially the part about being a foul-smelling baboon. I swallowed them hard as the Bitter Pill they were. Then Catfish Grimes made me roll over on my stomach, giving Lucy Featherdip the gun while he sharpened his knife. I figured him to cut my head off with it and kill me stone dead, so I took the Precious Time I had left to ask the Almighty to forgive me my sins in case I had done any, which I did not believe to be the case. I also said the Lord's Prayer and Now I Lay Me Down to Sleep, the last always being my Favorite.

Instead of cutting off my head, what they done was to tie me up, hands and feet, as tight as they could. I swear that they did not care if they cut off the blood or not or were risking giving me Gangrene. Then they got me up and hung me upside down from a low branch of a tree, with Catfish carrying me out so I would be over the edge of the creek.

"Now, are you going to tell us where your uncle's fortune is?" the Featherdip woman asked.

"Surely you jest," I replied, trying to act as if I did not at all mind being in a position in which my brain was working wrong side up.

"Let's just finish him off and be done with it," Catfish said, an evil sneer darkening his face.

"No," Lucy said. "Let us smear his face with fish grease and let the bears eat him. If no bears eat him by tomorrow, maybe he will be ready to tell us where the treasure is hidden."

Catfish cackled. Cackling is not a manly thing to do, and he sounded more like a beast than a creature whose ancestors came from the Garden of Eden.

Lucy wiped what was left of the fish across my face so that it would surely smell. Then she took the grease from the pan and rubbed it into my hair. Oh, the shame of it all as I hung, upside down and helpless. A tear formed in my eye and fell across my forehead. When they walked away, arm in arm, my heart grew heavy, for I thought my time had come.

THIRTEEN

WHEN THEY HAD gone, I threw myself about as much as I could, but to no avail. I could not free myself. Thinking how easily Catfish had lifted me to the branch, I wondered why he had not used his strength to do Honest Work and make a good citizen of himself.

Then I managed to take control of myself, as I was taught to do, and as I know my Dear Mother would have wanted. I had just convinced myself that I would think of something, something that would be both wonderful and ingenious, when I heard an awful roar.

I looked over to where the roar had come from and saw the worst sight I had ever seen in all of my fifteen years on this earth. It was a grizzly bear and her cub!

"Frolic!" I called out as loudly as I could. "Frolic, I need saving!"

I did not panic but a little.

"Frolic! Help!"

The mama grizzly reared back on her hind legs and kind of hissed at me, which I hoped was a friendly sign.

"*Frolic!*"

I heard a rustle on the other side of the clearing, and I saw Frolic coming through the bushes.

"What are you—" Just then he must have seen the bears because he stopped stock-still.

"Frolic, I would be much obliged if you cut me down from here," I said, in a polite manner.

Frolic looked at me, looked at the bears, and then turned and skedaddled into the woods.

My heart sunk in the upside-down position, which is a terrible feeling. I took a punch at the air in the direction Frolic had run and wished it toward him. Then I turned and looked at those bears and saw that the mama bear was coming toward me. She got real close and I closed my eyes, ready to meet my Maker. That mama bear started licking me with a tongue that felt like a metal file. I could only hope that she did not like the taste of Artemis Bonner.

Then she took a swipe at me with her big paw, catching me square in the hind parts and swinging me in that tree like a ball on a paddle.

Just then I heard some puffing and looked away from the mama bear to see Frolic coming again. This time he had found himself a long branch and had set the end of it ablaze. He pushed it toward the bear, and the bear backed off a few steps and let out a roar.

Frolic dropped the branch and moved off to the edge of the clearing.

"Frolic!" I spoke to my friend calmly. "The fire is right under me and I'm getting fricasseed."

Frolic came over and got the branch again and the grizzly started growling. He closed his eyes so he would not see the bear and held out the branch again. I hoped that my friend would not get eaten up by the bear, for good friends are hard to find. Although if things did not work out soon, it looked as if I would not need any friends, good or otherwise.

"WAAAA-OOOO!" Frolic screamed at the bears, trying to scare them away.

The cub jumped away and ran squealing into the woods, and the mama looked at it. I do think she was embarrassed that her cub had not eaten me and had instead run off. There was a shamed look in the eye of that mama bear when she lumbered off after her cub.

"Come up here and untie me," I said to Frolic.

Frolic looked over at where the bears had gone into the woods.

"You think them bears are coming back?" he asked.

"I do not think so," I replied.

I could tell that Frolic was not too sure about the bears, but he climbed into the tree and got me down.

It is not a manly thing to do to cry, but cry I did. The reason for this was that I was hurting something terrible and did not feel good beside.

"That's a smart thing you done," Frolic said, trying to make me feel better, "tying yourself up in the tree so that bear don't get you."

"I did not tie myself up in that tree," I said.

"That Foul Deed was done by Catfish Grimes!"

"He's got to be pretty strong."

I did not answer my friend but busied myself with Deep Thinking. My fight with Catfish Grimes and Lucy Featherdip had not been easy.

Now as far as I was concerned, the treasure could have been in Sacramento. But I did not want to have anything more to do with a place where bears trained their young ones on human beings, which I was. I contented myself with letting Catfish Grimes and Lucy stomp around in them woods if such pleased them. They had not found the treasure, but neither had I.

"Now what?" Frolic was sitting on the mule, and I was lying across its back because of the condition that bear had left my hind parts in.

"Lucy and Catfish have not found the treasure yet," I said. "But I do not care. I will go home to New York City and be done with this Awful Business."

"What you think I should do?" Frolic asked.

"I guess you must fend for yourself," I said, not looking at him.

Frolic did not say another word all the way back to Sacramento, and he did not look me in the eye either when we said our good-byes. But I was determined that it *was* good-bye, for things were not looking good, or even fair to middling.

FOURTEEN

THERE WERE TWO boats docked side by side, and I found out that one was going to Seattle, which was on my uncle's list, and the other one was going to New York City. It did not take me long to decide which one I would take.

"Captain," I said, "please take me to New York City so I can once again see my Dear Sweet Mother."

"I will do no such a thing," he said. "For you look like a diseased man and I do not want the likes of you on my ship."

I held down my temper and, drawing myself up to full stature, told him what had happened to my ear and my backside, and said that it was Villains and Evildoers that had done me in and not Disease.

"Then you are a jinx," he said, "and worse than the scurvy!"

I went to a small place that sold hard liquor and eats and ordered a plate of beans and a soda. When I looked up in the mirror and saw myself, I knew that the Captain was right. I looked more pitiful than a one-eyed mangy cat peeping in a seafood store.

But then a Voice come to me and said it was Fate that made me look so bad that I could not go home to New York. I was Destined to go on to the next place on Uncle Ugly's list, and the ship that would take me was waiting at the dock. It was an iron-bottom three-master that used to belong to the White Star Line and was now named the *Eastern Star*. I finished up my beans and soda water and went right out to make inquiry as to passage.

"For fourteen American dollars you can go all the way to Seattle if you are willing to sleep in the hold," the mate said. He was a red-faced man with chin whiskers that were neatly trimmed and an Honest cast to his eye.

"That suits me just fine," I said.

I looked to see what money I had left and saw that it was thirty-two dollars and nine cents. I knew what I had to do.

"How soon before the ship sails?" I asked the mate.

"Within the half hour," was his ready answer. "If you are not on board then, we will not wait for you."

"Be that as it may," I answered, "I must go find a friend and see that he has enough money for a decent meal and a place to stay."

"You're not talking about that fellow over there that's been watching you, are you?" the mate answered.

I turned around and saw that it was Frolic Brown himself. I walked over to him and saw that he was doing poorly, and that his handsome face was shaded with sadness. When I put my right hand on his shoulder, he lifted his chin and twisted his mouth up in his peculiar manner.

"Frolic, I have decided to go on to Seattle, Washington. I do not know what dangers lie there for me, or what Fate has in store," I said. "So I do not feel comfortable asking you to risk Life and Limb to come with me."

"I'll risk Life and Limb for you, Artemis," he said. "It's okay."

I could not answer his kind words, for

my heart was too full. Instead I put my arm around his shoulders, and together we walked to the ship that would carry us, like true brothers, to Seattle.

FIFTEEN

IF A TOWN COULD BE A bird or an animal, Seattle would be a sea gull. It did not as much mind what it was doing as take wings and fly. And just like a sea gull it took its own sweet time about doing anything. Since our funds were running low and I was not one to be either a Borrower or a Lender, I sought an honest job. Me and Frolic went from place to place and finally got lucky when we found work in a restaurant called Our House, an establishment owned by one Mr. William Grose. He was a big, good-looking man, with even brown skin, a white mustache, and white hair upon his head. He smiled a lot, even when he was trying very hard to work me to Death. But since it was a Colored restaurant, I figured that either Catfish and Lucy would come around to it or somebody who came to it would have seen them.

We got ourselves a room, also in an establishment owned by Mr. Grose, for a quarter a day and laid low until we got our bearings and my wounds healed. It was a good thing, too, because Frolic was acting poorly.

"Here, put this around your neck," I said, giving him the garlic I had put on a string. "It will keep the fevers away from you."

"Okay," he said. He put it around his neck and sat looking out of the window. The way he had his mouth fixed, I could tell that it was his Spirit and not his body that was ailing.

"You feeling low?" I asked him.

"Thinking about my mom," he said.

"What was she like?" I asked him.

"Real pretty," he said. A little smile came over his face. "One of the elders said that people got soft when they were near her."

"You remember how she looked?" I asked.

He opened his pouch and pulled out a small tin picture. On it was an Indian woman holding a baby in her arms. That baby had the dumbest grin I have ever seen on a Human Being.

"She is pretty," I said, not wanting to mention the Unfortunate baby.

"Yup," he said, showing me a grin that

looked a little better on him now that he had more face to spread it around.

He talked about his mom for a bit more, and when he went to sleep he was holding her picture in his hand. I made a silent promise to myself that when I got back to New York I would take my own Dear Mother to a studio and have our picture taken together.

The fifth day we were in Seattle, a man named Roscoe Dixon came into the restaurant. I served him a cup of strong coffee like he asked and went back to getting a chicken ready for the lunch meal. Frolic was washing down the counter.

"You see that hard character that was hanging around the oyster house?" Mr. Dixon called over to Mr. Grose.

"Half the characters around here are hard," Mr. Grose replied.

"This one's been around for a while, and he looks like a bad one," Mr. Dixon said. "Got a nice-looking woman with him, though. She dresses like a Christian lady, but I did not see either one of them in church."

I looked over at Frolic, but he was daydreaming and did not have his mind on serious business.

"They say what they wanted?" Mr. Grose asked.

"No, they did not," Mr. Dixon answered. "But the way I figured it, they must be looking for something. They're carrying digging tools and packing enough food to keep them going for two or three days at a time. They disappear once in a while, then they show up again."

"Is he carrying a gun?" I asked.

"Biggest gun I ever saw," Mr. Dixon said. "Keeps it in a strapped-down holster, too."

I knew I had to do some Hard Thinking. I had already put the onions and sausage inside the chicken, so I stuck it in a clay pot like Mr. Grose told me to, put in a cup of water, and covered the whole thing up good and tight.

"Make sure no steam can get out of that pot," Mr. Grose said.

I did not say anything to him in reply. I knew how to make Haunted Chicken, but I had other things on my mind.

I told Frolic what I had heard and saw that he was not too interested. I think he liked working in that restaurant. He had more of a liking for three square meals every day than he did for Adventure, but he did not back out of our Mission.

We laid low for a few more days until we spotted Catfish on the street.

"There he goes!" I said.

Frolic stood behind a post and looked around it. Catfish and Lucy were leading a mule down Commercial Street. Catfish was walking on one side of the mule and Lucy was promenading on the other. I could have taken a shot at them unbeknownst, but I had come to the decision that a different course of action was called for. I had already lost a nick from my left ear, part of my backside, and much of my Dignity dealing with Mr. Catfish Grimes, and that was all, the Good Lord willing, I intended to lose.

SIXTEEN

WE WENT DOWN TO A Low Dive near the wharf where they had a lot of fellows come in from around the city who liked to drink and fight. There was not hardly a day or a night that went by where someone was not getting to meet his Maker before he had a mind to. After taking everything in with a Keen eye for a full two hours, I went up to the roughest-looking man I saw. He was older than me, having reached his full manhood of Twenty-one, and a goodly brute of a fellow, six foot if an inch, Black as the Ace of Spades, and blessed with a face that would curdle running water on a clear day. I ordered lemonades for me and Frolic, and the stranger ordered a whole bottle of tequila for himself.

"There's a worm in that bottle," Frolic pointed out.

"Don't bother me none," was the quick reply. Then he took that bottle and turned it up to his head and drank half of it down.

I knew I had found the Right Man. I shifted my chair a little upwind of him and commenced my proposition. At first I tried being coy with him, pursuing the Gentleman's way of talking in polite circles and Beating around the Bush, but he would have none of it. So I, seeing this, came straightaway to the point.

"How much," says I, "would it take in U.S. Guaranteed greenbacks to get you to kill two people for me?"

"Five dollars," he said. He scratched himself a little and then said his price again. "Five dollars."

Seeing as how I was a working man, I found

that within my means and began to describe Catfish Grimes and Lucy Featherdip, whereupon he promptly upped his price to seven dollars, saying that if he had to look for *particular* people to kill, it would cost more.

We came to an Agreement on the price and shook hands on it. Right away I could see that beneath his sweaty shirt beat the heart of a truly honorable man.

Tracking down Catfish Grimes and Lucy Featherdip was not a hard thing to do, but I knew that catching them and giving them what for would not be at all a simple matter. Moby, that was the fellow me and Frolic had hooked up with, borrowed some sore-legged horses the next day, and we set out to find Catfish and Lucy.

Frolic did not cotton to Moby all that much and would not look at him full in the face.

"He looks hard," Frolic whispered to me.

It was a good observation and I meant to keep it in mind. Moby might have been honorable in the killing department, but I did not know that much about him, or even if he had come from a Decent home.

We came across the camp of an old, red-faced man whose lower lip was bigger on one side than it was on the other and made him look like he was in pain. We asked him if he had seen a man and woman who fit the description of Catfish and Lucy.

"Yesh, yesh, I sheen them," he said. He chuckled to himself until the chuckling turned to a cough, and then he stopped. "Durn foolsh, ish what they ish. Durn foolsh!"

"Why are they fools, sir?" I asked. I knew why *I* thought they were fools, but I wondered if he had a reason I had not considered.

"Becaush they'sh looking for gold and everybody knowsh they ain't no gold around here," he said. "Anybody who looksh for gold where they ain't no gold ish a durn fool!"

"What you looking for?" Frolic asked.

"I'm looking for gold," he said. "But I don't care if I find it or not. They wash digging here and there and looking over their shoulder like they had to get the gold out before shome other durn fool came looking for it."

I could not prevent a smile from crossing my face as I thanked the old prospector, for I knew why they were looking over their shoulders. It was the long arm of Artemis Bonner they feared!

We moved on awhile in the direction in which the prospector had said that Catfish and Lucy were headed, then settled our gear and found a place that seemed as good as any to set up a snare trap on the road. We were not going to depend on that trap alone but it would be a great help if it worked, I figured.

After we had set that trap, we sat down and waited. I asked Moby where he had got that name from, because it did not seem fitting for a fellow from this part of the world.

Moby did not reply to my question but just growled and spit on the ground. I refrained from asking him again about his name.

SEVENTEEN

THE SUN WAS hot and I had just about dozed off when Moby dug his elbow into my side. I opened my eyes wide and looked down the road from where we were hid in the bushes. Frolic was kneeling near and peeping through a bush. We were about thirty yards away from where we had set the snare. The road narrowed at that point, and I figured that Catfish would stay on it and walk into the snare rather than walk off the road, such as it was, and take a chance on the tall grass. From where I was I could see them, Catfish first and the woman right after. They looked tuckered from walking. When I saw them I had a little catch in my throat because I knew that the moment had come for Sweet Revenge.

Moby did not carry a gun but he carried the wickedest knife I had ever seen. It was long and curved and had two deep nicks in it. Moby ran his thumbnail over those nicks as we watched Catfish and Lucy walk toward the snare.

I could see Catfish and was glad he was in front. But he walked right through that snare and nothing happened. I was disappointed and was wondering what to do next, when Lucy Featherdip stepped into the snare and got jerked upside down in the air.

When this happened, Catfish Grimes took off running and hollering like a Wild Banshee. I started to tell Moby to go after Catfish, when something in the bushes caught my eye. It was on the other side, away from where Catfish had gone to, and I stayed low and pointed at it. Moby saw the grass move, and I guess he thought that was what he should go after. He took out that big knife and a look crossed his face that would have sent Death itself back into the shadows. Then he let out a screech and charged toward the moving bush.

For the first time in my life I could say that I saw a surprised look on an animal's face. The wildcat that sprung out of them bushes toward Lucy Featherdip turned toward Moby, and I could swear that if he could talk, what he would have said was, "Well, don't this beat all!" Moby's back was toward me, and I could not tell if he was surprised to see that wildcat, but it stood to reason that he knew he had not been invited to an afternoon tea. Anyway, the two of them, Moby and the wildcat, went around and around. They was clawing and gouging and biting at each other something fierce. I knew Moby was a tough man, but I did not know he was *that* tough. And let me say that the wildcat was not a slouch either when it came to putting up the Good Fight.

I snuck a look over at Lucy Featherdip, still hanging upside down, and saw that she was watching the fight, too. I did not want to look too close at her because, hanging upside down the way she was, her petticoats and bloomers were out in Plain Sight. Being the Gentleman, I turned my eyes away and stayed right where I was and watched the fighting between Moby and that wildcat, figuring not to get in the way while they were having at it.

For a while it looked like that wildcat was going to finish Moby off as they rolled around under where Lucy was. But then Moby got his arm free and the tide started to turn. Moby grabbed that wildcat by the tail and held him with one hand while he hacked away with the other. The wildcat was chewing on Moby's leg and clawing at his belly. Finally, Moby fell back away from the wildcat and that cat, knowing he had met his match, stuck what tail he had left between his legs and ran off into the bushes.

To be sure, Moby looked like something about to be hung on a meat rack. One arm was just laying at his side, and you could not see the front of his shirt for the blood. But he got up and started to stagger around some. When he got near to where Lucy Featherdip was hanging, she saw him coming and how terrible he looked and she let out a scream.

"Catfish! Catfish!" she called out. "Ca-a-at-FISH!"

In all the excitement and everything I had forgot about Catfish Grimes. He came out of the bushes and lifted his gun.

"You done whipped that wildcat fair and square," Catfish hollered out, "and you done a good job at it. But now your time has come!"

Without saying another word, not even a by-your-leave, he shot Moby. Moby, he looked down to where he had been shot and pushed at the place with his hand like he was trying to push off the hurt spot. When he done this he looked just like a hurt buck and my heart truly did go out to him.

Catfish had seen what Moby had done to the wildcat. He had seen that big cat running off licking his wounds, and he knew that if Moby got his hands on him, it would surely be the end of Catfish Grimes. So he lifted that pistol again and shot Moby until there was not any bullets left in the gun. Moby did not stand but for a second more and then fell back stone dead. This made my heart heavy, for the Lord said, "I have no pleasure in the death of him that dieth," and neither does Artemis Bonner, unless it be in the death of a Foul Person.

Then Catfish put down the gun and went to haul down Lucy Featherdip. That was when I realized that what with everything going on, Catfish Grimes had not seen me, either. I did not say a word, for the time was past for mere Words and exchanging the pleasantries of the day. I got up and run across at Catfish Grimes. I grabbed him by the hair and gouged him in his eye with my thumb. He let out a yell and we got to getting at each other.

EIGHTEEN

NOW, I AM NOT the kind of man that likes to brag upon what he can and cannot do. But I must say that I am a Hard-Fighting man and do not lay down before no one or turn tail and run unless the odds are at least three to one, or unless I am the one without a gun in a gunfight. Other than that I do not seek quarter from any man who is born natural.

So whatever Catfish laid on me, I laid the same on him and more. And, although I am a Christian man and do not like to indulge in the

Rough Stuff, I was not too unhappy about beating up on Mr. Catfish Grimes.

I had him sunk to his knees and was gouging at his eye again when he commenced to pushing me backward. That did not bother me none, because I figured that I would be able to get his eye out soon and then the fight would be mostly, if not all, in my favor. But what I did not know was that the filthy beast that was fighting had a dirty plan. He was pushing me back so that Lucy Featherdip, still hanging upside down, could get ahold of me. What that putrid, duck-livered, twice-rotten woman did was to clamp me good around the head and chomp down on my good ear. When she did that, I let go of Grimes and tried to punch her on the jaw.

Let me tell you that it is not easy to punch someone on the jaw when they are hanging upside down and chomping on your ear. Catfish rolled away and started looking around on the ground for his gun. All the time he was going through his pockets looking for his bullets, too. I knew that if he found the gun, he would blast me to Kingdom Come. I tried choking on Lucy Featherdip the best I could, but I soon knew it was no use. That woman was as hard to put down as any two men I had ever fought. There was only one thing for me to do, and I done it.

I jerked my hand away from her and let myself fall right to the ground, leaving that woman with nothing but a mouthful of ear. Then I went after Grimes again. I knew he was no match for me. I banged him a good one to his nose and he went to howling. I was just about to kick him in the top part of his head when he charged into me. His pointy head went right into my belly, and by the time I had got my breath back again, he had pushed me back to where Lucy Featherdip was hanging. She grabbed me again and Grimes went after that gun again. Old Lucy was getting weaker from hanging upside down, and she did not get a good grip on me this time. I broke loose from her just as she was clawing at my face. I half ran, half fell over to where Catfish was. I brought up my Dukes and he brought his up, and then I kicked him on the knee as hard as I could, and he fell backward and landed hard.

From the corner of my eye I saw Frolic waving a stick.

"Whomp Lucy!" I called to him.

I ran over to hold Lucy so Frolic could whomp her, but she grabbed me by the hair and twisted me just at the right moment so that Frolic hit me instead of her. My knees got real weak, and it would have been all over for me because Lucy was swinging toward me with Murder in her eye, but Frolic caught one of her petticoats and swung on that so's she missed me.

I saw Catfish crawling around, dragging his leg which I kicked, and looking in the grass for his bullets.

"Come on, Frolic!"

I turned and ran off as fast as I could, and Frolic was right at my side. A shot whistled past my head, and I tried to split up from Frolic so we would not both get killed, but he stayed with me. After a while, just when I thought for sure my lungs would bust out of my body, I turned back and saw that we were clear of Catfish.

If truth be known, things were getting pretty discouraging. I had paid good money to have these two polliwogs killed. It had been cash in advance, too. I figured Moby must have died with the money I give him still in his pocket. That was just as good as if he did not have it at all, for Artemis Bonner did not take money from the dead unless he had a bona fide I.O.U. paper. Catfish Grimes probably took the money off Moby's body anyway.

We found one of the horses and got ourselves back to Seattle and went to the Grose barber and undertaker shop, where an old Colored woman put a poultice alongside my head where Lucy Featherdip had bit off a Goodly portion of my good ear. She told me to take a drink of Rum, but I am a member of the Temperance Union and am not taken to Strong Drink nor Late Hours. We did not want to go back to our room because the roaches in Seattle were bigger than the water rats in New York City, so we went back to the restaurant and each of us had a bowl of navy bean soup to get back our strength.

"Now you got a nick on one ear and the other ear is near chewed off," Frolic said. "You were almost killed."

"No thanks to you," I said. "You were the one that hit me in the head with the branch."

That hurt him and he cast his eyes down, and I did not give a Hoot for I was really mad.

When we finally went back to our room, I was aching so bad that even places I did not even own were hurting. I gave Frolic a "good night," but it was not friendly.

The funny thing was that, even though she was a hellion and one of her eyes had a mite more squinch than the other, Lucy Featherdip was not what you would call a bad-looking woman. And her voice was low and sweet. But she was so ornery that just thinking about her made me shake like an old hound trying to pass a straight razor in a snowstorm.

Lighting out after Lucy Featherdip and Catfish Grimes was beginning to tell on both my brain and my body. It was clear to me that I had to bring my Powers of Concentration to this job and let nothing lead me astray.

When we went back to work for Mr. Grose, he thought it game to make light of my chewed-up ear.

"Whatever was chewing you up must have spit you out because they didn't like you," he said. Then he laughed with his belly shaking, and all the people sitting around trying to bum a Free Meal were laughing, too.

But Artemis Bonner was not laughing. He

was checking his uncle's list of places and becoming more Steadfast in his ways and in his Character. We stayed in Seattle another week or so until I got myself healed up pretty good from my chewed ear and a case of the runs, and then we booked passage to Anchorage, in Alaska Territory. We had decided to put off bringing Catfish and Lucy to the justice they deserved and find the treasure first.

NINETEEN

ANCHORAGE, ALASKA, was as cold as a Gravedigger's heart. There was no nook or cranny that the cold did not find you out, and the wind was worse than the regular cold. It cut through you like a knife and made you feel like a Homeless Orphan. If any place on earth was cold, then Anchorage was colder. Plus it was a miserable place not fit for a Human Being. They didn't have anything that you could call a regular street and the buildings were plain out ugly, but in the distance they had some mountains that were just about the prettiest you wanted to see. I reckon that's why Mr. Seward bought the place from the Russians, al-

though to be sure there were enough mountains down in the regular United States.

"It ain't really all that bad," a little short fellow by the name of O'Hara told us. "It just gets
a little colder at night than it does in the day-
time. Anyway, if you get lucky you might find
gold or even diamonds and get rich overnight."

"Did you get rich overnight?" I asked.

"No, I did not," he said, a wistful look in his
eye. "But I come close once. Found the biggest
hunk of gold ever found in these parts. It was so
big, it took two horses just to drag it around
town."

"What happened to it?" I asked.

"Tried to get it weighed so I could sell it,"
O'Hara said. "They didn't have a scale big
enough in Anchorage to do the job. I had to
drag it clear over to Selkirk."

"Did they weigh it over there?" I asked.

"Sure they did," O'Hara said. "What you
think I drug it over there for?"

"What did they say it weighed?" I asked.

"Well, there's two kinds of gold, hard gold
and soft gold. The soft gold is the best kind, and
the kind that big old nugget was made of. Like I
said, it was too big for anything to carry, so I

had two horses drag it from Anchorage to Selkirk. As I dragged it, the gold started wearing away from the scraping on the ground. By the time I got to Selkirk, it was only half the size it was when I started and it was *still* big enough to make me the richest man in the territory of Alaska.

"But by the time I dragged what was left of it back to Anchorage, there was only a little piece of it left. Piece about the size of a baseball. That was just enough to pay the fellow for letting me use his horses."

That was indeed a Sad story if it was true, but it was not why me and Frolic were in Anchorage. We were on a Mission.

"Do you know your way around these parts?" I asked O'Hara.

"That I do," he declared. He stuck his little finger into his nose, twisted it around a bit, then wiped it off on his chest. I know that he did not learn that in Sunday School.

"Well, I am looking for the grave of my dear departed uncle," I said, not wanting to let him on to the Real Thing. "Here is a map of where he is buried."

He looked at the map and commenced to

scratching his head. I figured he was either stumped or lousy and I moved away a mite.

"Where did you get this here map?" he asked.

"From my aunt, who kept it in a copy of *The Pilgrim's Progress*," I said. I had thought about saying she had it in the family Bible, but I did not want to bring the Bible into a lie.

"Your uncle must have been quite a man," O'Hara said, "if he drawed up a map of where he was going to be buried."

"If you can take me to the place on this map marked off with an 'X,' I will give you a five-dollar gold piece," I said. "And that is the promise of a man who believes in the Good Book."

"Mostly I am too busy to do anything like that," he said. "But I will not be too busy tomorrow, so I will go with you."

Me and Frolic went looking for a place to stay, and he picked out a place that looked likely and we went in. It was an outrageous place with a lot of Hard Cases sitting around a pot-belly stove. Me and Frolic got a room but had to pay the dear price of one dollar cash money. We got a small room in the corner, a bottle of water to drink, and a pail of washing water.

"You got a picture of your mum?" Frolic asked when we had settled down in our room.

"No, I do not," I said. "But when I get back to New York City, I will have a picture taken."

"She nice?"

"Frolic, my lad." I took off my shirt and began to wash, especially under my arms, which were beginning to smell in an Unsavory Manner. "All mothers are sweet and Wonderful."

"I wonder what Catfish's mum looked like," he said. "Maybe like a alligator with long hair and teeth."

I wished to defend the institution of Motherhood, but in Catfish's case I could not think of anything to say that was kind, so I did not say anything.

We did not sleep but a few hours because of the short blanket they gave us and the bodacious bedbugs. It was plumb cold in that room, and the wind whistled through the cracks around the windows something terrible. I tried to fall asleep so I would not think about the cold, but every time I dozed off, the bedbugs would bite me and wake me up. I was not sure if the morning was going to find me froze to death or eat up by those bugs.

We set out early, taking with us a hunk of pan bread that was left over from the hotel's breakfast. O'Hara led us this way and that way, and all the time he mumbled to himself so that I thought he was Daft.

We looked high and low and pigeon-footed our way around so many sides of Anchorage that I thought I knew the whole place by Heart. If there was any place in or near Anchorage that could have been where my uncle Ugly had buried that treasure, we must have looked at it. But what we found was nothing. We did this for two whole weeks before we gave up the search and a good bit of the money that Frolic and me had earned in Seattle.

TWENTY

I WAS NOW AT THE Low Point of my life. The only other places marked off on the map was Tucson and Tombstone, which were both back in Arizona Territory. If Catfish and Lucy had gone there instead of wasting their time coming to the territory of Alaska, they might already have the treasure and all I would get is a Cruel Blow from the hand of Fate.

There was a rowdy hall in Anchorage called Senator C.W.'s, and me and Frolic found ourselves sitting in it listening to the piano player.

"I hope he plays 'Beautiful Dreamer,'" Frolic said.

"He is an Alaskan," I told Frolic, "and these Alaskans are mostly heathens and have probably never even heard of 'Beautiful Dreamer.'"

"Some of them are Indians," Frolic said.

I looked around and saw that some of the Alaskans did look like Indians, which was a big surprise.

We were fast running out of money and there were no jobs to be had in Anchorage, and so it looked like we were going to die in a place that did not even have the God-given decency to know the songs of Stephen Foster. In my unhappy state the notion come to me to tuck my tail between my legs and Give up the Ghost, but I did not want Frolic to know how low I had sunk.

I went on a few days like this, in a state of Deep Depression, thinking of my failed Mission and the disappointment I would cause my mother, and wondering what to do. Then one night we were sitting in C.W.'s sharing a tin plate of baked beans and a piece of meat that was accused of being mutton but was definitely Not Guilty, and I looked to see if the cook was still wearing his shoes.

Over the bar there was a picture of a melancholy girl, naked from the ground up to her knees but with a sweet face and soft brown eyes. Me and Frolic were not doing much in the way of the talking department and so I looked up into the eyes of that Melancholy Girl in the picture and I saw them blink. I dropped my fork and looked again. Then I saw that they were not real eyes but reflected eyes on account of the glass they put over the picture to keep the fingerprints of the unsavory-type patrons off the girl. I did not do anything at first but to continue to eat the beans. But I confess the chewing was easier than the swallowing.

"Frolic, get ready for action," I said softly.

Then I turned slowlike and caught the eye of a Sallow youth staring at me. When he knew that I was onto him, he stood and started toward the door.

"That fellow was eye-balling me too hard for it to be mere chance," I said to Frolic.

"He better not mess with us," Frolic said. I saw that he was ready for a good fight, and so was I. We watched as the stranger left the hall, and throwing two bits on the table for the grub, we followed him outside.

He looked like he might break into a run, but I was soon at his side and laid a heavy hand upon his shoulder. Frolic jumped right in front of him and stuck his chin less than an inch from his chest.

"Sirs," the youth said, "do not harm me, for I am just a poor orphan who means no man ill upon the face of this earth. May my poor dear mother perish if aught but truth passes my lips."

"I believe you mean me no harm," I said to him, putting a hard edge to my voice, "but I also think that you know more than the names of the Saints in Heaven."

"And he got a pistol in his pocket to blow a hole in you about this big," Frolic said, holding his hands about a foot apart. "Or maybe this big." He held them a little closer together.

"My companion is right. If you do not tell me your business straightaway," I said, "I will have no choice except to blow you to Kingdom Come."

"Sir . . ." He commenced to tremble, and I told him to take hold of himself.

"You have nothing to fear if you tell the Truth," I said.

"In that case I will speak it gladly," he said. "I was hired by a gentleman and his lovely wife to follow you and report to them your whereabouts. This I have been doing for four days."

"And describe this pair to me," I said.

"They are black like yourself, sir, and the man has a scar upon his forehead and a big nose, sir."

"And the woman?"

"An average sort," the youth said, "although one eye has a bit more squinch to it than the other."

My heart was lifted with the light of Glad Tidings and Joy. Catfish Grimes and Lucy Featherdip were indeed in Anchorage.

"And what are they doing?" I asked.

"Right now they are not doing too much," the youth said, "for the woman is laid up with a frostbit toe."

Taking the youth by the collar, I had him show me the cabin in which Catfish Grimes and Lucy Featherdip were staying. Then I bade him never to let me gaze upon his features again, for fear of Bloody Death. I looked him straight in the eye as I spoke these words so that he would know I meant Business. He was only too glad to flee with his life.

"What we going to do?" Frolic asked.

"We need a strategy," I said. "They know we are here and maybe have plans of their own."

TWENTY-ONE

WE WENT back to our room and saw that the door was Wide Open and all our possessions gone. Frolic started to bawling and carrying on, and we were in a terrible way when the owner of the hotel showed up at the door carrying our stuff.

"Why are you making such a noise?" he asked. "You are disturbing my other guests."

"Because we have been robbed," I said. "And our privacy invaded."

The hotel man looked around the room.

There was nothing in it but a bed, a chair, and a dresser with the basin on it. "A fellow not much older-looking than you was here before," he said. "Said he knew you and went into your room and took some things. Threw most of them outside on the ground. Here they are. If you are broke, I will give you a full dime for the picture of the Indian squaw."

Upon hearing this glad news, Frolic jumped up off the bed and snatched the picture of his mother from the fat hands of the hotel owner. I saw that my gun was gone and so was a plug of worming tobacco.

When the hotel owner left us, I chastised Frolic on how easy he had cried, and he allowed as how that was true.

"I don't know how much more fighting with Catfish and Lucy I can do," he said.

Frolic was getting tired of the fighting and so was I, but I was still determined. I sat down and let my brain race with figuration. If someone sent by Catfish and Lucy had searched our room, they must still be looking for the treasure.

"We got to go right now to face down Catfish and Lucy," I said to Frolic, "and let Boldness be our Guide."

Frolic looked at me and smiled, but I saw that it was a smile that was hard in the making. "You sure you want to go along with me?" I asked.

"I'm sure," he said.

He did not say it too strongly, but I had to have my young friend with me. We had become a team and True Friends to boot.

It was cold when we set out. But we were warmed by the Rightness of our Mission, and thoughts of Justice and Good Doing came to my mind.

"There is a window in the back, and you go around there and break it," I told Frolic as we approached the door. I had secured a stout axe handle that I proposed to put to good use. "When I hear you break the window, then that will be my signal to go into Action."

"They gonna be sorry they tried to get the picture of my mum," Frolic said, a steely look in his eyes.

He grabbed a rock and moved slowly around the side of the house, and I went to the front door. In a minute I heard the back window breaking and I got ready. As I figured, Catfish

Grimes came popping out with his gun drawn and at the ready. I knocked the gun out of his hand with the first blow and with the second whomped him soundly across the face.

Catfish let out a bellow that sounded like something you would hear in a hog-slaughtering contest, but I did not show mercy upon him. I hit him another stout blow that caught him on the chest, and he fell over backward and let out a moan and then flopped around a little and was still.

"Do not take my life," he said, "for I am a reformed man."

I did not believe that a man like Catfish Grimes could reform so quick. But I have a Tender heart and I went up to him to look into his eye to see if he was telling the truth. When I did this, he grabbed me around the ankle, shouting, "Lucy! Lucy! Come get the gun and shoot his fool head off!"

When he said this, I gave him a double-strength whomp that would have caused Serious pain to a dead man and which made him let go of my ankles. He tried to stand and run, but I would not let him get to his feet. He crawled like the wretched raccoon he was all the way back into the cabin with me on his tail whomping to Beat the Band. I knew he would remember the whipping I was laying on him for many a day. All the while I was keeping an eye out for the Featherdip woman. She was sitting up on the bed with her foot propped up on a pillow looking like a fancy lady. I whomped Catfish Grimes once more real good. In the eye blink when I had looked at where I was whomping Catfish in the head, Lucy had grabbed the oil lamp and was fixing to throw it at me.

Little did Miss Featherdip know that it was me, Artemis Bonner, who had made careful plans this time. For in through the back window hopped none other than Frolic Brown, and by the way he moved, you could see that he was mad.

That oil lamp came flying across the room, and it took all of my efforts to get under it. It crashed into the corner, which burst into flames. The room filled with smoke.

"That's it!" Lucy cried, and she started off the bed after me.

Just then, Frolic reached her and grabbed her around the waist. She pulled back and boxed him soundly on the ears. By this time

Catfish had pulled himself up and got me in a Death Grip around the waist. I had no choice but to get him in a Death Grip around the top of his big head, and we were holding each other as best we could. But the thing that got my attention as much as anything was the fight between Frolic and Lucy Featherdip.

For every time there was more than two inches between them, Lucy would give Frolic a smart blow to the head. The little fellow was not faring well. He had to push his head against her bosom and try to stay too close for her to pound on. Lucy was trying to push him away so she could punch him, but then Frolic stomped on her toe something awful.

"IIIIIEEEEE!" She let out a scream that stopped me and Catfish cold.

On one side of the smoky room it was me and Catfish holding each other and wrestling around without too much moving around.

On the other side, Frolic had both of his arms around Lucy's waist and was busy trying to stomp her on her frostbit toe, and she was busy hopping and lifting her feet so they looked like they were doing the Back Country Two-Step. Except, of course, they did not have music and Lucy was still hollering.

"Ca-a-a-atFISH! Ca-a-a-atFISH!"

I had a good hold on Catfish, and I knew we would surely prevail with a little more time. But we did not have the time, because I knew it would be only a few minutes before we would all be roasted.

"Frolic! Make for the door!" I called.

Frolic danced Lucy over to that door just as nice as you please and gave her a push backward, and she landed hard on her bustle.

I let Catfish's head go and threw a few punches, and as soon as he let me go to return the favor, I broke for the door as well. Catfish tried to get after me, but Lucy caught him as he ran past her.

"Don't you leave me in here!" she was screaming at him as me and Frolic escaped from that fiery Inferno. We stopped a little distance down the road and saw that Catfish had pulled Lucy out and they were both sitting on the ground looking like the cowardly coyotes they were and holding their hurt parts.

Me and Frolic took our Own Sweet Time going back to our room and said "Howdy" to one and all with smiles on our faces, for we had done well.

TWENTY-TWO

WE DECIDED that Uncle Ugly's fortune was not in Anchorage, for he would not leave it in a place where so many desperate people were and would not want to go back there under any circumstances. And of all the placcs I have been, I can say with a straight face and a Pure Heart that I did not like any of them as much as I liked America. I figured that Uncle Ugly must have left his fortune in Arizona because they have Civilized people there and not Cutthroats, Heathens, and Foreigners.

As soon as I could sit up good without much hurting, me and Frolic went down to the docks and looked for a boat on which we could work our way back to California.

"Artemis, you beat up Catfish, and he's a grown man and pretty mean-looking," Frolic said.

"I did not think that you were suited to the Hard Life," I said. "But the way you laid into

Lucy was truly something to behold."

"I was just more scared than she was," he said, sporting a grin that put me in mind of his baby picture.

We got a job on a steamer from Anchorage and had to clean out the Captain's quarters and serve him three times a day. Frolic got seasick and stayed that way all the way, just changing from green to white and back to green, depending on what time of day it was. I thought a lot about what we had been through and how much I hated Catfish. But when I thought about Lucy, I knew I did not hate her as much as I did Catfish and was even getting used to her low-down ways.

"You think we ever going to get that treasure?" Frolic asked.

"Frolic," I said, "I have been stomped, whomped, cooked, frozen, beaten up, almost eaten up, and worked harder than a blue Georgia mule all for that treasure, and now I want it!"

I knew that foul Greed had tainted my youth, but I looked forward to the way of Easy Living. It was a good thing to think about even though I knew that it was harder for a rich man to enter the Kingdom of Heaven than for a camel to pass through the eye of a Needle. Still, it was a sore but stubborn Artemis Bonner that helped his friend Frolic off the boat in San Francisco. The flesh was weak and getting weaker but the Spirit was willing.

TWENTY-THREE

THE San Francisco dock was as busy a place as I had ever seen in my life. There were ships of every kind and wagons stretched from the water to a good two miles away.

On the dock there were men pushing and grunting and sweating the sweat of Hard Labor. Black men worked right next to whites, and there were Chinese all over the place. There were also a great many children, some just running around and others having a game of catch.

"Would you like to play with them awhile?" I asked Frolic. He was, after all, still a mere child.

"I'm hungry," he said.

At first I was surprised, but when I looked close at him, I saw that his look had grown sharp and his Attitude serious.

"Hey, get out of the way!" a drover yelled at us, and nearly ran us down.

We stood aside and gave him hard looks as he passed us by.

We found a diner, and I ordered fish stew.

"What you want, honey?" The waitress had a kindly face but only two teeth in the front of her mouth.

"Apple strudel," Frolic said.

"This ain't no fancy restaurant," the woman said. "You can get fish stew, fried fish, crabs, and oysters, and it all comes with bread."

The fish stew was not bad as far as I was concerned, but Frolic did not find it to his taste. When the bill came, I saw that it was not to my taste either, and we were soon to find out that San Francisco was no place for a poor man.

"We are going back to Tombstone," I said, as we walked along the dock. "I believe that is where my uncle has hid his treasure, and that the map was just to throw off the Wicked."

"Which is Catfish Grimes," Frolic said. A sailor had given him a cap, and he wore it low over his eyes.

"Do not forget Lucy Featherdip," I added.

"For although she is of the Weaker Sex, she is as guilty as any man."

"She ain't weaker, either," Frolic said.

We got tired of walking on the dock and went to a shipping company to book passage to Tombstone. The little bald man behind the counter looked us up and down and went back to reading his newspaper.

"You boys looking to get to Tombstone?" a tall white man with a mustache asked.

"That is our destination," I said.

"Well, in four days there's a coach headed from right aside this office, and it's headed to Arizona Territory," he said. "If it is not full up, you can probably get a ride for five dollars each. Tell the driver I said it's okay."

He gave me his card, which read *George W. Parsons*, and shook both my hand and that of Frolic in a Manly fashion.

We did not have the five dollars each and went searching for Honest work. When we found a way to make a day's pay for a day's work, it was not all Milk and Cream.

Near the waterfront we found a job stretching hides for a tanner, and I do not mind saying that it was the worst job that I have ever had. It was not so much the work itself but the smell was enough to turn a Dead Man's stomach. Besides that we had to walk two miles twice a day back and forth to the room we had rented.

Our one comfort was that we knew that Catfish and Lucy would not be doing much high stepping, not with the whipping we had put on them in Anchorage.

When the four days were up, I was glad and Frolic was more than that for he was not used to hard work. We got to the place to get the coach and saw that there were nine people trying to get on, and the driver said that only eight could go but then found out that only six of us had the Cash Money.

We rode the first leg of the journey with three good nuns on their way to Los Pueblos. I have always been partial to the Church and to people who have devoted their lives to the Good Book. So I was very hurt when they began to look at me and Frolic with Disagreement in their faces just because of a little smell from the tannery.

"Is there something wrong?" I asked.

"Thy garments do not smell of myrrh," one pretty little Sister said.

Which was surely true, but not the subject of polite conversation, so I gave her a look of Stone.

When we came to the next rest stop, two of the nuns had a chit-chat with the driver, and for the rest of the trip me and Frolic had to sit up top with the baggage.

"You always stink like that?" the driver asked me.

"Only when I am about to shoot somebody," I said without a drop of humor in my voice, "does the smell come upon me."

"You smell like you fixing to shoot the whole United States Army," he said.

I was sorely taxed at such a statement and did not answer.

TWENTY-FOUR

TOMBSTONE was a rough town with a lot of shooting and stabbing going on but not a whole lot of outright killing. There was talk of the Stockton gang coming over from New Mexico, but the talk sounded more like Sport than news. On Main Street there were a lot of bad-looking cowboys who did not do much of anything except drink and fight and some miners who did the same.

I had thought that Uncle Ugly's treasure was pure gold nuggets or a pile of gold coins, but the talk around the city was there wasn't any gold in Tombstone or near about, only copper. I couldn't see anybody getting too excited about a copper mine, so I kept looking for gold.

"Why don't you leave the map here?" the sheriff said. "I'll ask people who come by here if they know anything about it."

"No, sir," I said. "I will take it with me and figure it out for myself."

I had been warned not to think too highly of Mr. Earp, the sheriff, although he looked like a True Gentleman.

"Another colored fellow was through here a few days ago with a map that looked like yours," the sheriff said. "Must be a run on those maps."

I knew it had to be Catfish, and I got a feeling like the bottom of my stomach had just fallen out. My mind was fixed on doing the Right Thing, but I must confess it was getting harder. I began to think of that cactus, the bear, and my chewed-up ear, and I was not sure whether or not I wanted to go through it all again.

"I guess we got him again," Frolic said, looking me square in the eye.

"I guess we have," I said, knowing that he was feeling the same as me. But want to or not, facing Catfish was something I had to do. I had not rode out to my aunt's place to tell her that I was back. I needed some good news to give her, and if it could not be to hand her the gold, then it had to be to tell her that I had got rid of Catfish and Lucy.

There weren't many places in the West with a whole lot of people, especially a whole lot of women. Tombstone had a lot more men than most places, but still didn't have many women. I asked around if anybody had seen a man with a big nose and a woman with one eye a little more squinched than the other. The only woman who fit that description was No-Nose Mary, an Apache woman who came from someplace near Tempe. I said the woman I was looking for was not an Apache as far as I could tell and she had a nose.

"She got a pretty nose, too," Frolic said.

I did not comment on this remark by my young friend but knew it to be the truth.

There was a man who did odd jobs down at the O.K. Corral, and I was told that if anybody knew anything about strangers in town, it would be him. We went over to the Corral and I asked him if he knew my uncle.

"Ned Bonner?" The old man wore a tattered butternut jacket and dark pants into which he tucked his hands when he talked, like his fingers were cold or something.

"That was my uncle's name," I answered.

"He wasn't the best-looking fellow in the world, was he?"

"No," I said. "But he was honest and God-fearing."

"Well, I knowed him pretty good," he said. "He used to bring his horse in here to bed him down sometimes. Mostly he used to come into town to talk to a lawyer fellow named Marcus A. Smith, over there on Tough Nut Street."

We thanked him kindly and went over to Tough Nut Street, which was in a section called Rotten Row. Rotten Row did not look so bad to me. The houses were adobe and not too unpleasing to the eye.

"There it is." Frolic pointed to a sign on the side of a building.

We went up the stairs and knocked on the door and found Mr. Smith sitting with a shotgun on his lap. We showed him the map, and he looked at it this way and that and then looked at us.

"This is not an assaying map," he said. "This could be a homesteading map, or maybe it's a well someplace out in the desert."

I told him I was obliged to him for what he had said. He looked like the crafty sort to me and talked like he had a mouthful of maple syrup. There were very few men I trusted, and he was not one of them.

"Can you give us the name of a good place to rest our heads?" I asked.

"You can try Dommer's," he said, smiling. "Most of the roaches there will give you a fair shake."

Dommer's was a good choice, for it was only twenty cents a day and for an extra ten cents you could use the bathtub.

"That's in the morning," the woman who ran the place said. "In the afternoon after everybody's used the tub, it's only two cents, but the water ain't hot."

We did not see neither hide nor hair of Catfish and Lucy for four days, and I had to admit to Frolic that I was Perplexed as to what to do about finding my uncle's treasure.

"You think Catfish found it?" he asked.

"I can only hope that is not the case," I said.

On the fifth day both me and Frolic decided to take baths, which we had not done very often. The tub was down on the first floor, and we had to take our clothes down there, which was better than having to carry the water up to our floor. Frolic went first and he scrubbed down good, using a small brush and brown soap. He dried off and put on his pants and shirt.

"Maybe I should shine my shoes," he said.

"Frolic, you are turning into a Dandy," I said.

I was sitting in the tub washing my feet when that lawyer fellow come into the room.

"Why, you are the fellow who showed me that map a while back," he said.

"That is right," I said, not liking to do no whole lot of conversing when I was Naked as a Jay Bird.

"Another fellow come into the Courthouse yesterday asking about a map, and I took a look at it and it looked just like the one you had. I told him I had seen the map before, and he described you like a picture. Tell the truth, I don't think he has a particular fondness for you, either. Soon as he started talking about you, he put his hand on his gun."

"What did this fellow look like?" I asked.

"He looked kind of under the weather," the lawyer fellow said. "And he was not as handsome as some men I have laid eyes on."

"Was he alone?" I asked.

"He was," came the answer. "But outside the Courthouse I saw him walking with a woman with a gimpy leg or maybe a hurt foot."

"Lucy!" Frolic's voice cracked.

"Just thought I would let you know," the lawyer said.

He started peeling off his clothes, and I figured he was next in the tub.

I hopped out of the tub, drying myself with one hand as best I could while I put on my clothes with the other. Catfish and Lucy *had* made it to Tombstone. We got up to our room as quick as we could, looking both ways as we did.

TWENTY-FIVE

ALL THE back and forthing with Catfish and Lucy had driven us to a state of Nerves. That night we took turns sleeping, and even when I slept I did so with One Eye Open.

"I wish we'd found out about Catfish when we was dirty," Frolic said. "You feel tougher when you're dirty."

That was indeed the case, but it was already too late. We got up early and went downstairs and ordered a good breakfast of grits, fatback, and biscuits in redeye gravy while we made plans.

"We should sneak up on them," Frolic said. "Then we can get them before they get us."

That was the first time I had heard Frolic say anything about Catfish and Lucy getting us. I thought to put his mind at rest but could not think of anything but Catfish standing in the courthouse with his hand on his gun.

"Maybe you should stay away from me awhile," I said. "In case they catch me Unawares."

"Might as well stay with you," Frolic kind of mumbled. "Got no place else to go."

When the food came, I put on a smile for Frolic, but the swallowing was still hard. I started jawing about what I was going to do when I got back to New York City to get my mind at ease, when suddenly Frolic's eyes grew big as saucers. I put my fork down and turned around as slow as I could.

A cold chill run through me as I gazed upon the form of Catfish Grimes standing in the doorway.

"You got your gun?" Frolic whispered.

My lips tried to say no but nothing came out.

I did not have my pistol, not liking to take it with me to a meal where I would say Grace. But I wished I had made an exception in this case, because I knew that Catfish had the Upper Hand.

"Artemis Bonner," Catfish called out, "is that you in there?"

"It is none other," I declared.

"Well, I am calling you out," Catfish said. "I mean to meet you in the street when the sun reaches high noon. Then we can settle this thing Man to Man."

"It would have to be Man to Humpback Rat-tlesnake," I said, "because you are the lowest thing I have ever seen."

"Will you face me down?" Catfish called out. "Or are you just a yellow-bellied she-dog with a face like the hind parts of a gray mule and more woman in him than Real Man?"

Hot anger rose up in me and I had a mind to go after Catfish right then and there. "You name the place and I will be there," I called out.

"Right out front," he said. "I will come down the street from the cemetery end, and you can come down from the other end."

"That is fine with me," I said.

Some cowboys sitting around having their morning coffee and a chaw commenced to making bets on who was going to die that day.

Now I was not afraid of Catfish Grimes, but I did not trust the sneaky Salamander. I did not take my eye off him the whole time he was standing there in the doorway. Even though I did not trust him, I knew that him calling me out was a thing of Honor and I was still a man of Honor. I had never Faced a man down before. I did not shirk from what I had to do. Catfish was tired of me dogging his every footstep, and I was tired of doing the dogging.

I looked up at the Seth Thomas clock on the wall and saw that it was two hours before noon. From where I was sitting I heard some of the betting, and it was mostly in favor of Catfish, him being the one who called me out.

"I got two dollars on the one with his nose chewed off!"

"I got a dollar on the one with his ear chewed off!"

"I got a dollar says that they both get killed!"

"Yeah, but which one you bet gonna die first?"

"Artemis," Frolic put his hand on mine, "you ever have a shoot-out?"

"No, I have not," I said. "But if you go upstairs and get my pistol, I will do my best."

"I don't think it's a good idea," he said. "They're betting and stuff."

"I know," I said. The betting did not make me feel too good, either, for I did not like listening to speculation as to how I was supposed to get shot up. Then some fellows came in and I could see they was asking for me 'cause the barkeep pointed over to me.

The first fellow was tall and skinny and looked like he didn't spend no whole lot of time in the sun.

"You the fella in the gunfight?" he asked.

"I am that man," I said.

"Well, I run a little funeral parlor and shoe-repair business across the way. Now if you give me four dollars, I will see to it that you are put away decent in a near-white shirt and clean hands, including the fingernails. If you don't get killed, you get three dollars back. The barkeep, he said he will kick in fifty cents for a shave and a haircut just 'cause you're bringing in so much business. Taking a good look at you, though, I don't even think you'll need a shave."

I gave him the four dollars, because if by some Turn of Fate I did get myself killed off, I did not want to lie in the street like a stray while Catfish was in the bar with Lucy on his lap talking about how he done it.

"Artemis." Frolic spoke in the softest voice I had ever heard him use. "I think we should run away."

"Frolic, if I ran away, I would never again be able to look a Real Man in the face," I said.

A truly fat fellow came up to me and looked

me over close.

"I have bet ten dollars against you and I want to know if my money is safe, for I am a Family man and cannot stand no big losses. You ain't no gunfighter, are you?"

"I cannot tell you that," I said. "For I have never tried the sport before. As far as I am concerned, it is in the Hands of God Almighty, who judges all things!"

"Thank you, son, that's just about what I wanted to hear," he said. "My money is in good hands."

I was beginning to think that I had made a mistake. I do not like to be the underdog in a two-dog race, especially when there is only going to be one dog to do the "tale" wagging.

Frolic and me went up to our room. My friend was sad, and I did not want to let him down by getting myself killed.

TWENTY-SIX

WE HAD NO sooner got into the room than a knock came on the door.

"Speak your mind!" I called out.

"I am a friend and mean you nothing but some good," the voice came back.

I had the pistol ready when I opened the door in case it was a Low-Life trick on the part of Catfish. In front of me stood a big Black man in a United States Soldier's suit.

"I do not have much time," I said, "nor do I bother with matters that are trifling. So if you have a piece to speak, go on and speak it!"

"My name is Charley Slade," he said, "and I have bet my last two-and-a-half-dollar gold piece that you are going to win the fight today. It is not a lot of money but all I have in the whole world. You look like a good sort to me."

"You are also a wise man, sir," I said, "and I will try not to disappoint you."

"The only thing that gives me a fret is that the fellow you will be facing down has the biggest gun I have ever seen. I came to bring you this Colt .45, which is a really good gun."

"Take it," Frolic said.

I took the Colt and shook his hand warmly. He was a gentleman and a Credit to his Race, which was also mine.

When the time came for me to meet Catfish, I walked slowly down the stairs and Frolic walked behind me. He had the other gun and said that if he saw Lucy Featherdip, he might shoot her On Sight.

That Colt had more weight to it than I expected. I stopped to strap it to my leg and took my good time doing it to give my knees time to stop shaking.

"Artemis . . ." Frolic started to say something but could not bring the words to his lips. He patted my shoulder with the gentle touch of youth, and I knew he was the best friend I had ever had, for he had faced Danger with me and even Death.

It was a sunny day, and when I got in the middle of the street, I had to squint to see good. Frolic stood on one side, and I was glad to see him there. I was about to put on a Mean Look when I noticed that I was standing in front of the Bird Cage Saloon. It was the very spot where Catfish had brought an end to the life of Uncle Ugly, and the thought of it nearly took away my breath.

It wasn't but a moment before Catfish showed up with Lucy Featherdip sashaying by his side. When he stepped out into the middle of the street, she went and sat on the edge of the water trough, very ladylike.

"There's an extra two bits in it for you if you shoot him in the head, Catfish," a man on the side called out.

The Black fellow that had given me the gun called out for me to shoot fast, because he could not afford to lose.

"Neither can I," I said.

"When I count to three," Catfish called out, "go for your gun!"

Soon as he said "one," both of us drew. Now I was not much of a fast draw, but I was ready that day to kill Catfish Grimes. I shot two times and he clutched at his chest, and a look of Death come on his face. He turned a little bit and his gun went off just before he fell to the ground. There was a splash and I turned to see Lucy Featherdip fall back into the trough, felled by her Partner in Evil. People started paying off their bets, and the undertaker came and drug off Catfish.

Lucy Featherdip was only touched on the arm by the bullet, but it served her right. When you lay down with Dogs you get up with Fleas. The fellow who gave me his gun came over and patted me on the back and gave me a dollar from his winnings besides.

"It is a good thing you are on the side of Law and Order," he said.

Which was true.

When I got to Frolic, there were tears in his eyes, and we hugged and shook hands and then hugged again, for we were as happy as we could be.

We went back into the hotel and had two cold lemonades and took some slaps on the back. Frolic was happy that I had won, and I was happy that I would see the Light of another Day.

TWENTY-SEVEN

ME AND Frolic had done in Catfish and were pleased to get the Good News that Lucy had lit out for parts unknown. My aunt heard the news and came into town to see us.

"Why did you not tell me that you were back in Tombstone?" she said.

"Because no news is better than bad news," I said. "And I have the bad news that I have not found Uncle Ugly's treasure."

She gave out a heavy sigh that nearly broke my heart but then lifted her head bravely.

"Then I must find my treasure in the rewards of a Christian life," she said. "But my heart is made lighter by the fact that you have sent Catfish Grimes to his Reward, and may his miserable butt sizzle in the Fires of Hell forever."

That was a truly tough destiny to wish upon a man, but I could understand that it came not from my aunt's heart but from her Grief. Me and Frolic stayed with my aunt for another week, just resting and leading the Soft Life, which we richly deserved. We had played our hands as best we could, but it was cruel Fate that played the last Ace. Frolic got along with my aunt right well until she started talking about how he should take a bath once a week.

We said our good-byes to my aunt, took the stout lunch she provided for us, and boarded the train headed back east.

"So what you gonna do?" Frolic asked as we settled down in our seats.

"Go back to New York City to be with my Dear mother," I said.

Frolic did not speak but only looked out of

the window at the crowd of boys and girls who had come down to the station to see the train off.

"You boys got tickets?" The conductor stopped and looked at us.

"We would not be on the train without them!" I said, giving the man our tickets.

He checked them, punched them, and handed them back.

"What are you going to do?" I asked Frolic.

"I don't know," Frolic said. "Maybe learn a trade."

"We got tickets to Chicago," I said. "I'm going on to New York City from there. Why don't you come with me?"

"They got Cherokees in New York?" he asked.

"None to speak of," I said. I noticed that he had put a big smile on his face and a twinkle in his eye, and I knew we were headed to New York City together.

"What can I do in New York?"

"Everything there is to do. With a new hat and a store-bought coat you could be a big-city man like me," I told him. "New York City has more sights than all of Tombstone and San

Francisco put together, plus it is a Safe place to live."

Frolic looked out the window as the train pulled out. Some kids ran alongside and waved and he waved back.

We got to New York, and I was so glad to be home, I said a fond "How do you do?" to every man, woman, and child we met. My mom was pleased to meet Frolic, and he seemed just as pleased to meet her, and I knew me and him would be lifetime friends and brothers.

I told my friends that the United States and the Territories of the West were mighty rough and that I had been forced to shoot a man myself. Naturally, I told my mother that it was in Self-Defense, which was the Gospel Truth, so that she would not think I had become a bad case.

"And I like your friend," she said, referring to Frolic, who had secured a job with me working for the Great Atlantic & Pacific Tea Company.

This is where the story would have ended had it not been for a letter I received just when the memory of my adventure had been put behind me and I had settled down to the business of Life. I could not figure out why I had got a letter from Lucy Featherdip after all these months. But when I read it, I got a great shock to my heart and a bad feeling in my stomach as well. This is what the letter said.

Dear Mr. Artemis Bonner,

I am writing to you to inform you of the Truth, which is what God loves and which is what every true believer must live by. The Truth is that you have been plotted against and are the Victim. When me and Catfish Grimes came back to Arizona, we were sorely used and on the brink of Despair which no kind word or deed would make better.

We decided that you were too tough to kill even though you were a puny little thing. Catfish said that ugly men did not die easy, and in your case I could see that it was true.

So Catfish and I decided to leave you alone and just look around for the treasure. And much to our surprise we found it and great it was, too. But we knew you were going to be on our trail soon. So

Catfish plotted up with another man to make you believe you had killed him. The man gave you a gun with bullets that did not have enough powder in them to hurt even a baby. And to boot Catfish had some tin under his vest and his long johns to cover up his heart.

So everything was going like it was supposed to. But then Catfish shot me, hitting me in the right arm in a most soreful and hurt way and knocking me over. That was not part of the plot at all. When I came to my senses, he was long gone. It is my understanding that he wanted to kill me and run off with another woman. Now he is a rich man off your uncle Ugly's treasure and is living high on the hog here in Emporia, Kansas, with a slightly cross-eyed woman named Annie Hartnett. This is a wrong thing to do and that is what God knows as well as me.

I have got better from being shot, but I do not get around too good from the way that mean little white boy you had with you done stomped on my frostbit toe. But I

do not bear a grudge and hope you feel
the same. What I am saying is let us let
Bygones be Bygones and do what is right
by killing Catfish Grimes and Annie
Hartnett. Then we can get the treasure
and I will be your woman.

Signed,
Lucy Featherdip

P.S. You can even bring that mean little
white boy and I can introduce him to my
sister Flossie.

I still had the gun that fellow give me, and I jumped up and got it. I emptied my slop pail and turned it upside down and shot it. That bullet bounced off the slop pail like it was a rubber ball.

If there is anything I cannot stand, it is a man what gets other men to lie and do their evil for them, which is what Catfish plainly did. When a man has somebody else lie for him, he is spreading evil the same as Satan and is a sore to the sight of the Righteous.

So now I am bound and determined to kill Catfish Grimes and so end the Devil's work once and for all, and when I told Frolic he spat on the ground, which is not Sanitary but which shows that he Means Business and will go with me to do what we must do. As for the Hartnett woman, I will let Lucy Featherdip work that out between herself and her Conscience once we team up.

I feel some pity in my heart for the woman who is with Catfish Grimes and privy to his Evil ways, but I know that evil follows evil, and that what must be done must be done. And to show the world my good intentions and kindly nature in this matter, I have wrote down here everything that has happened so that the Gentle Reader, knowing what has happened to me, can see the Truth, close the pages, and say a hale and hearty Amen.

AMEN.